# HAWKSMOOR
## OF PARADISE ROW

**By the same author**
*Swift Books*
Genius at Work
Sky High

*Leopard Books*
Sparrow
The Whistler
Free-Wheeling

*Tiger Books*
Good for Kate

*For younger readers*
Natasha's Swing
Natasha's Badge

© Veronica Heley 1989
First published 1989

ISBN 0 86201 543 X

Line illustration on page 4 by Bert Hill

Phototypeset by Input Typesetting Ltd, London
Printed and bound in Great Britain by Cox and Wyman Ltd, Reading

# HAWKEYE
## OF PARADISE ROW

## Veronica Heley

**Scripture Union**
130 City Road, London EC1V 2NJ

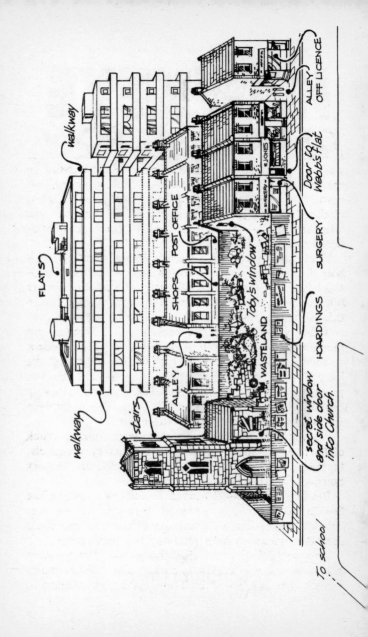

# 1

It was another Do It Yourself move. Their ancient car was loaded to the roof, and overhung with furniture on the roof-rack. Their mother, Kate Webb, changed gear with an effort, impeded by all the black plastic bags of clothing on the front passenger seat. The rented van swerved into the kerbside in front of them, and shuddered to a halt. So did they.

'Well, this is it!' said Kate, smoothing her short dark hair. She looked around with pleasure at her new territory. She was the new Youth and Community Worker for the Paradise Estate, and boy! Was she going to make things jump around here!

Toby, scrunched in the back under two large pot plants and the cool-box, took one look out of the window and wished he'd stayed in bed, thank you. Why did she have to pick such crummy places to live? Their last place had been bad enough, but this was the pits. Every building was marked with graffiti, and the pavements and alleys were ankle deep in rubbish.

Above them towered a bleak nineteen sixties block of flats, with windy walkways and blank-eyed tunnels. Opposite were streets of dreary nineteenth century housing. There wasn't a tree in sight.

Beside Toby, Nikki heaved herself up, pushing the box of groceries onto Toby in her effort to get out. 'Phew!' said Nikki, plopping out of the overloaded car onto the pavement and stretching, like her mother.

Toby and Nikki were twins, though you'd never guess it to look at them. Nikki was dark and built four square, just like her mother, while Toby was fair and looked as

5

if you could break him in two between your finger and thumb.

Toby waited to be let out. The catch on the door his side didn't work. Trust Nikki to have grabbed the side where the door opened. She said it was because she'd be travel sick otherwise, but Toby knew it was because she was a lot better at getting her own way than he was.

Mother and daughter stood with their hands on their hips, and their chins thrust out, surveying the promised land.

Old Ben, who was one of their mother's special clients from way back, got down from the Drive Yourself van, and opened up the back. Toby inched himself over the seat and out of the car, depositing his various burdens on the pavement.

Kate was already unlocking the door between a doctor's surgery and a dirty-looking newsagent's. The flat above the surgery was to be their new home. They'd been living in council accommodation ever since they could remember, ever since the twins' father had been killed in a car crash when they were little.

Nikki said she couldn't remember their father, and Toby couldn't really, either, but he could remember the terrible rage his mother had gone into when she'd heard. He still dreamed about that, sometimes. The doctors said his asthma had started then. The doctors usually went on to say how lucky it was that Nikki took after her mother, strong as a horse, never a day's illness, what a lucky girl you are, then!

Toby didn't hold it against Nikki, but it did sometimes cross his mind that she'd grabbed all the luck in the family. Everyone liked Nikki and admired her. Toby tended to get sat on.

Like now. He carried the heavy box of groceries up the stairs after the others, even though it hurt his arms and back and made him start his gasping act. The others told him crossly, that he shouldn't have bothered, and asked why he'd left the plants on the pavement. Then they said would he find the front door key which his mum had put down somewhere and couldn't find. They called Toby 'Hawkeye' because he was good at finding things.

The flat was pretty awful, he thought, but there were big windows at the back and front, which might make up for it. The flat was really a maisonette, on two floors. His mother grabbed the big bedroom overlooking the tiny yard – which she called the 'patio' – and Nikki said she'd better have the other one on the first floor because it was next to the bathroom.

That left two rooms on the top floor. One was a sort of junk-cum-attic room largely occupied by water tanks, with only a cracked skylight for a window. But the other room was Something Else.

Toby couldn't believe his luck in getting this room. It was an odd shape and the roof came down low on one side, so you couldn't stand upright there, but it had two great big windows, one overlooking the back yards of the houses opposite, and the other . . .

Toby disturbed a pigeon which had been sitting on his window-sill, and it whirred up and up into the sky above. Toby had never seen so much blue sky in all his life. It seemed to go on and on and up and up for ever. The sun was coming through the window and making him feel warm for the first time for months.

'What a dreary view!' said his mum, appearing with Ben and unrolling a square of underfelt and then a thin second-hand carpet.

'It's marvellous!' said Toby.

'Do you mean that old tower?' said Ben poking his head out of his balaclava like a tortoise. 'Or them there flats? Or is it the dump site that's taken your fancy?'

Toby hadn't noticed the tower, nor the flats, though now he came to lower his sights, he could see that the block of flats did loom over the houses to his right. And down below there was a great stretch of derelict land surrounded by hoardings.

'Squalid,' said his mum, looking over his shoulder. 'Ought never to be allowed. I'm not having you two playing down there, do you hear me? I'll get on to the Council about that straight away.'

She went off muttering things like 'Hazard to health', and Toby could see what she meant, now he'd taken a proper look at it. Pure grot.

Ben was still peering over his shoulder. 'Looks like it was a pretty big church there once, might have come right up to the wall of this place. Explains why there's no windows looking out this way on the first floor. This window must have been above the roof level of the church.'

'What do you think happened?'

'Bombed, most like. You can see the old tower's still there, and a bit of the main building. They'd call that part the nave.'

'Like Knave of Hearts?'

'Can't spell, so don't know. You can see how they've bricked it off, rough-like, and fenced off the whole area with those hoardings. Probbly they don't know what to do with it. Probbly they thought they'd rebuild, or sell that bit of land off. Must be worth something. Your mum's right. Don't you go playing down there. It's dangerous.'

Toby hung out of the window. There were fragments of walls standing here and there on the site, maybe to the height of a tall man. There were shrubs growing around and in among them, but you couldn't really call it a nice place, because somehow or other people had found their way in through the hoardings and dumped rubbish. Old beds, bikes, and bins. Plastic sacks, gaping with torn sides. You name it, they'd got it. Including broken-backed armchairs.

'Lockjaw,' said his mum, heaving a roll of bedding

into the room. 'That's the least you'd get, if you cut yourself on one of those rusty tins. You hear me, Toby?'

'I hear you, Mum.'

'And do your Hawkeye act, will you, and find the kettle? I thought I'd put it in the box of groceries, but it isn't there.'

'I saw it. You put it on the window ledge.'

'Right, then get moving. Nikki's bringing her chest of drawers up, drawer by drawer. Ben'll give me a hand with your bed, and you can put your clothes in that cupboard in the wall. Gracious, better get the dustpan and brush to it first. You can do that, can't you?'

'Yes.'

He hated being the weakling of the family. It was all wrong that Nikki could heave stuff around like she was Superwoman, and if he lifted so much as a chair, he had to sit down and rest or reach for his inhaler.

He swept out the cupboard and used his inhaler, and tried not to let them see how the dust had choked him. It was nice in that room, and the sunshine helped a lot. The doctors were always saying he'd do better to eat more and fuss less, and then he'd grow a big strong boy, and he did try.

But he took after his father, who had apparently been a picky eater, too. When they sat down soon after to a microwave meal, Toby just couldn't eat. Nikki finished his helping.

Toby trailed up stairs and down, carrying up his books and arranging them on a couple of planks held apart by bricks. They fitted nicely into the space where the roof came down to meet the floor. His bed was set up under the big window overlooking the waste ground, because that was where it got most sun. There wasn't anything else in the room, except for an old scratched desk that had once been his father's, and a tin trunk, likewise.

Nikki came up to see if he'd got more than his fair share of anything, and was pretty scathing.

'What a dump!' she said, looking out of the window. 'Why don't they pull that awful tower down, and build some nice houses? There ought to be a law.'

Toby felt protective towards that tower. 'It was a church, once. I don't think you can knock down churches, just like that.'

'But they did, didn't they? There's only that silly tower left. Why not make a clean sweep? No-one uses it. Look, it's all boarded up, windows and all. What use is it?'

'It's got a gold ship on top. See? On one corner of the tower.'

'Whatever for? It's not really gold, is it?'

'No, I don't suppose. It's a weather vane. Shows which way the wind blows. Look how the sun shines on it.'

Nikki removed her attention from the tower, looked round the room, and satisfied herself that she'd got the better of the bargain by moving in downstairs. She said if he wasn't coming down to watch telly, Mum thought he'd best get to bed early.

Toby lay down on the bed, thinking he'd undress in a minute but he wouldn't be able to read in bed because his bedside light had got broken in the move. Luckily the nights were getting shorter.

The sun slid off the edge of his bed and he reached for a jumper to put on. The next thing he knew he was pushing aside a loose section in the hoarding down below. It was almost like a door. He slid through, into the Wasteland.

The sun was still shining and it was so warm he thought he could hear bees at work among the flowers. Roses were throwing trails over the stumpy ends of walls, and shrubs were coming into bloom. Daffodils were breaking open, standing in clumps in the grass.

A man was bending over, tapping with a hammer and nails, doing something to a stretch of trellis work.

The man looked up and said, 'Hi. Come to help?'

10

# 2

In his dream Toby could feel the sun on his face. He felt as if he were lying in a shallow pool of warm water at the sea-side. He was smiling, feeling happy.

He opened his eyes and the sky was grey, looking in on him. All grey, as far as he could see all the way up from the block of flats opposite. Those flats were like the side of a huge ocean liner, with lots of portholes and with the walkways outlining different decks.

There was a tantrum going on downstairs. Nikki and his mum, of course. He sighed, and then he remembered the garden below, and sat up to look out of the west window.

It wasn't there.

Just the dump.

He couldn't believe it. The garden had been so real. He had gone in and talked to the man, and they'd agreed the soil was a bit on the poor side, but with a bit of fertiliser here, and a bit of watering there, the roses would be a great show.

Only there weren't any roses there at all, not now. Nor daffodils, nor even any grass. Only weeds and rubble and rusting heaps of junk. Disgusting. A skeleton-thin cat was foraging among the dustbin bags.

'Get up, Toby!' That was his mother, getting into her yelling mood.

Toby jumped out of bed and reached for his clothes. Then he realised he was fully dressed, except for his shoes. He must have gone to sleep thinking about the dump area, and crawled into bed some time during the night, without really waking up. He thought he'd better

11

not tell his mum, or she'd shout even more. He changed his shirt quickly, found his tie, and went downstairs to the bathroom to wash and tug a comb through his hair.

The tantrum had reached the sulky stage.

His mum always wore a boiler suit in some bright colour for work, with Doc Martins and an Army surplus jacket if it were cold. Nikki couldn't see why she shouldn't do the same for school. She hated wearing a skirt. Usually she wore Toby's cast-offs, because although he was taller, she was fatter and it about evened out as to size. He wasn't hard on his clothes, not like most boys, and she looked good in them, and knew it. Every time they started at a new school, they'd have this argument about her wearing shorts and every time his mum would throw a wobbler and she'd win, of course, in the end. Toby couldn't think why they bothered to go through the motions.

He got the yoghurt, the muesli and the coffee out and set the table for breakfast. The pop-up toaster was awkward. He couldn't manage it, so he put out the special diet rolls and the marg instead. Their mother wanted to see them safely into their new school before she reported for work at the council offices, and she didn't have any time for frills.

She said, dropping them off outside the school, 'Now kids, listen; I'll get another key cut for the front door today, but till then you'll have to get the spare from the man in the newsagent's who's been looking after the place. I'll try to be back early, but if not, get something out of the freezer and put it in the microwave, will you?'

She drove off, the big end on the motor clonking away as usual. She'd got a bet on with Nikki that the car wouldn't last till the end of the month, and what they'd do about a car then, she couldn't think.

'Come on, then!' said Nikki, as usual more than willing to plunge into the hurly-burly of the new school. 'We'll miss play, if you don't hurry up!'

'Coming,' said Toby, checking he'd put his inhaler into his school bag.

She pushed her way into a group of kids, and he soon lost sight of her. Now and then he could hear her voice raised as she claimed it was her turn for whatever game it was they were playing. Toby stood back and watched for a bit. They were early. He quite liked being there early, and able to suss the place out a bit.

The school was part ancient and part modern. Some of it looked all right, but most of it could have done with a lick of paint or a plain, straightforward job of demolition. Toby wished he were back in their last school, which he'd not liked much at the time, but in retrospect it had been marvellous.

Starting in a new school was pure grot.

A bell went, and everyone rushed into the school buildings. He followed at a safe distance from a group of rather large and boisterous boys. It would be just his luck to be in their form. He could feel his chest getting tight and squeezy, just thinking about it.

He *was* in their form. The form master was all right, sort of, with one of those heavy laughs which didn't make you want to join in. The lessons were all right, too, he supposed, not difficult anyway, and they didn't seem to have done anything he hadn't.

Then it was out in the playground, and the gang crowded round him, as he'd known they would. When they got so close they were breathing on him, Toby tried to back away, knowing that any sign of fear would make them redouble their attention, but feeling himself begin to wheeze. They laughed. One pushed him on the shoulders. A second kicked out at his legs. They told him to turn out his pockets. They wanted his dinner money. They took it, and said he'd better bring some more tomorrow, or else.

Toby realised they thought he was a coward and could be bullied into doing whatever they wanted. He wasn't a coward, but he knew he was weak. In the old school he'd had a couple of friends who'd stood up for him, and he'd got along all right, keeping himself to himself and 'not noticing' if the baddies terrorised any of the smaller kids.

In his first school it had been the same. It seemed that wherever you went there were baddies, and this time he was up against it without any friends.

'What you doing with my brother?' demanded a furious voice. Nikki burst into the group, all elbows and feet in heavy shoes.

Nikki wasn't afraid of anyone or anything. She swung her school case against the shins of the biggest boy, and told him to lay off her brother, or else!

The biggest boy swore, but one of the others laughed, and that set them all off, roaring with laughter, falling about and propping one another up.

'And sucks to you, too!' said Nikki, red in the face. She seized Toby by the hand and towed him out of the way.

'Thanks,' said Toby, feeling awkward, and hating himself for having to be rescued.

'Don't mensh!' said Nikki. She looked around for her new friends and darted off once again into the crowd.

Going home, Toby followed Nikki and her new friends at a safe distance. Nikki had passed him by without even a wink when they left the school, so Toby knew he wasn't to claim her acquaintance just then. That was OK with him. He felt battered enough as it was. There was always so much to take in, when you started a new school. Nikki and her lot crossed the road and went into a sweet shop. Toby went on down the road, keeping the church tower in view. The sun hadn't come out today, but he knew he was travelling in the right direction because the block of flats loomed on the horizon like a dark cloud, and the church tower stuck up in front of it, with its bright gold ship on top.

'There he is! Grab him! Let's make him jump!'

The gang were some way behind but they had got him in their sights and they were going to run him down. It was their way of having fun.

Toby guessed they lived in the flats. He thought if he could only get to the newsagent's and get the key to the flat first, he'd be safe. He picked up his pace, but some of the gang broke away, crossed the road, and started running. They were going to cut him off.

He plunged through the traffic across the road. He was right under the tower now, but of course the hoardings went all round the site. There was no cover there.

He looked over his shoulder. The traffic was holding the others up, but he didn't have time to get to the newsagent's, get the key, and get off the street.

He remembered the bent-back bit of hoarding. Had that been a dream, too? If so, he was cornered and done for. But if not, if the bent bit of hoarding were really there and he could slip through into the Wasteland, then he'd got a chance. He couldn't remember where the break in the fence had been. He slid along, his back to the hoarding, pressing against it.

The gang were yelling and jumping up and down, trying to get through the traffic. Any minute now they'd be across and . . .

A double decker bus swung across the traffic, hiding Toby from the gang, and at the same time he felt the hoarding give way behind him, and he tumbled backwards into the Wasteland.

The hardboard flap closed behind him, but he wasn't safe yet. If anyone would know about that flap, they would.

The place looked strange, like a moon-struck, moon-mad landscape. It had begun to drizzle. The sky was empty.

'Help me!' cried Toby to someone, somewhere.

There wasn't anyone about, of course.

Slipping and stumbling, he made his way into the corner between the hoarding and the tower. He could see the window of his own bedroom high above his head, across the Wasteland. Perhaps if he could crouch down under some tarpaulin . . . but there weren't any tarpaulins here. Someone had had a picnic, and built a fire. He could see the charred remains.

He was trapped in that corner. The hoardings didn't have any other gap in them. He went all round the tower. Odd, unexpected bits had been built out here and there. A grating struck loud underfoot. A doorway leered from a dark corner. He tried the door. It was locked. Beside it was a low window, not large, and not far off the ground. Once it had been barred, but the bars had long since gone, as had the glass. A piece of ply had been nailed over the gap but rain, or possibly a tramp in search of a night's lodging, had so worked on the wood that it was jammed across rather than fitted tight into the frame.

Toby wrenched it out, hoisted himself in, and crawled into the tower.

He pulled the piece of ply back into place and held it there, waiting. Would they discover where he'd gone? If they did, then there was no way he could save himself.

# 3

Toby could hear them outside, shouting to one another, asking where 'that rat' had gone.

Toby shivered, clutching his knees, feeling his chest grow tight and his breathing thicken. It was very dark. He was sitting on a stone stair, by the feel of it. The boys crashed around outside for a while and then gave up. But they didn't go away. Toby could hear them settling down for a good old natter and perhaps a smoke. They sent someone to fetch cans of Coke and some chips. They were going to be there for quite a while, and there was no way he could get out without their seeing him.

Toby was miserable. He hated the new flat, and the school, and the boys. He hated everything, including himself.

Last night in the garden . . . but there was no garden. It had all been a dream.

A very odd dream. He'd never had one like that before. It did him good to think about it, even now. The man had been so kind, so strong and skilful with his hands, and yet so shabby and tired. Perhaps he was a tramp, a tramp who used the church to sleep in.

No, he hadn't been real, because the garden hadn't been real. Only, somehow, it had been more real than the Wasteland. Toby couldn't get the man out of his mind. It wasn't only that being in his company had made Toby feel good, but it was also the things he'd said. Stirring-up words, they'd been, about not letting the weeds take over your life; and that the Wasteland was a battleground, and it could go either way, to good or evil. Then there'd been something else, something which

Toby couldn't quite remember now, but which had made him think very hard at the time.

Groping about in his mind, Toby thought the man made him think of the teacher in his old Sunday School. Not that it was 'his' Sunday School, precisely. Sometimes Kate had off-loaded her kids onto friends for a weekend, when she had to go to a conference or something. Toby had had this one really good friend, Jack, the sort you could say anything to.

Jack and his family usually went to church on Sundays, and although Kate had sniffed about it, she hadn't objected, so Toby had gone, too. He'd gone quite a lot, even when he hadn't been staying overnight with Jack. He'd enjoyed it. He'd liked the singing, and he'd liked the stories about Jesus. He'd got a sort of shopping list of things he wanted, and he'd told Jesus about them, and sometimes they'd come true. Jack had said shopping lists of prayers were for beginners and there was more to prayer than that. Toby didn't know what Jack had meant. Wasn't it OK to pray for things you wanted?

That was about as far as it had gone, until he'd moved.

He'd taken it for granted, going to church, and being with people who loved Jesus. He hadn't thought of it as something he really needed; more of an optional extra, like school trips, or music lessons.

Then he'd moved and everything had been horrible and he'd felt a great sense of loss. It was like treading water, not knowing how deep it was, not knowing who to clutch on to.

There was no Jack now; only the gang.

He couldn't go back to the old church, and there was no church here. Worse, there was the shell of a church here to remind him of all that he'd lost, but it wasn't in working order. He felt more than a sense of loss, he felt he had a grievance about that. It ought to be there!

He needed it.

The man in his dream had tried to tell him something

18

about the church, but every time Toby thought he was catching the drift of it, the words slid away into the darkness. He simply couldn't remember, but he knew it had been important.

He was getting cold, sitting on that stone step. He had put his school bag under him, but the cold was coming through that, too. The gang was still outside. His eyes had got accustomed to the light now, and it seemed to him that it was darker below, and lighter above. Perhaps if he climbed the stairs he could find a window and signal to Nikki to fetch his mum.

He went up the steps on his hands and knees, feeling his way. He didn't have to go far. The light grew stronger. He'd come to a door on a landing. The door was ajar. He pushed it open and went in.

And then there was space and light.

What an odd place, thought Toby. So high, and so wide and nothing in it except rubble and a couple of rotten old pews. The floor was tiled, mostly, but the tiles were cracked and looked scorched.

Of course, this was the back part of the church. That door behind him would once have let onto the outside world, through the bell tower. That breeze-blocked wall ahead was where the rest of the church had been knocked to pieces. The church started out at one end, and came to an abrupt halt. Where the altar should have been, it wasn't. And there were boards nailed over the places where the windows had once been.

It was a mess.

And cold, too. He hugged himself, dancing from one foot to the other.

He couldn't go out yet, so he might as well explore. There were some doors at the back of the church, let into dark oak panelling. The first one opened easily, and gave him a fright, for out fell some mops and buckets and cleaning rags which had been pushed in there long ago, and forgotten. Above them were stacked vases and pedestals for the flower arrangements which had once decorated the church.

Toby was in anguish lest the boys outside heard the noise, but apparently they didn't. He left the things where they were and tried another door. This one let onto a small dank room, with rows of hooks around it, and a deep cupboard, now empty. Perhaps the choirboys had kept their robes there. Perhaps it had been the vicar's office. There was a door leading outside, but it was locked.

There was a third door, in the corner, and Toby really had to struggle to get that one open.

More steps. He went up them fast. It was getting lighter, the higher he got. The steps went round and round, and he was beginning to feel he wouldn't make it when suddenly he tumbled through into a weird sort of loft.

Enormous timbers crossed the tower at this point. Perhaps they'd have hung bells from them once upon a time, but there were no bells there now.

There was still glass in these windows, and it was a lot warmer than downstairs. Perhaps the sun was going to come out, after all. Toby rushed from window to window, all four of them, one on each side. He could see their own flat, and he could see the boys gathered in a clump down below, looking like plastic toys from this height.

He could see right across to the flats, and even along the walkways that led to them. He could see way down the road to the west, as far as the school. He could see into all the backyards and terraces, and into several shops and bedrooms. It was terrific.

He couldn't see his mum, nor Nikki, but for the moment he was safe and didn't bother about getting rescued.

There was a ladder leaning against one corner, leading up into a hole in the roof, but when he tried it, a rung broke. It was too dangerous to go any higher.

Perhaps this was where the tramp had lived. There was a rickety old camp bed in one corner, with some mouldering blankets on it. There was an old chest of drawers, a faded rug, a cupboard and a broken chair, all no doubt thrown out of somebody's house years ago, and long since forgotten. There was a pile of old hymn books, musty and torn, and some children's Bibles and drawings. It was a junk room.

Toby liked it a lot.

He sat on the bed, but it was so dusty that he started coughing and had to use his inhaler. No tramp could have slept there, not in all that dust, not for years.

He held his breath, and tipped the blankets into a corner so that he could lie down on the bedframe and there, wedged into the corner behind the bed, was a dirty, cobwebbed old exercise book. Toby flicked it open, seeing pages of notes, with dates, like a diary. It was pretty old. He dropped it onto the floor and dived for something else, something that had been under the diary.

It was an old leather case, the fastening rusty with disuse, but Toby had seen that shape of case before, and with any luck . . . yes, there was a really truly pair of binoculars in the case!

Now he could see everything. He really was Hawkeye, now. He was so high up in the tower that he could see every detail of the pigeons that were clustering and clucking around the ledges. He was getting a real bird's eye view.

He got the binoculars focussed, and an alley across the road, which had been just a fuzzy blur, shot into sight. It was one of the alleys which led to the shops from the block of flats and yes, there was a little old lady, toddling along with her basket on wheels. She was counting over some money, lots of notes, and pushing them into her purse as she went.

And there, peering round the corner of the alley at her, were two youths, one black and one white, both wearing scruffy jeans and T-shirts, watching her as she paused to push her purse down among the groceries in her shopping basket. She must have just collected her pension from the post office on the corner.

Suddenly Toby realised what he was looking at. He was watching a robbery about to take place.

He shouted out to the old woman to take care, but he was too far away, and she'd didn't hear him. He looked right and left, willing a policeman to come walking down the road, only of course they usually went around in cars nowadays, didn't they? Wasn't anyone going to help that poor old woman? What would happen if the lads did take her money? Would she starve to death?

The lads were sliding along the wall of the alley, stalking her. She was plodding on, head down, pushing at her shopping basket. She wasn't very steady on her legs. They'd only have to give her a little push, and she'd be over on the ground, quite helpless.

Toby couldn't bear to watch, and he couldn't bear not to.

Suddenly there were two more people in the alley, coming towards the woman. They were a middle-aged couple, rather large and stout. They stopped to exchange a word or two with the old woman, whom they obviously knew. The two lads stopped hugging the wall, and pretended they were just strolling out, taking the air and all that. The three stood there, chatting. The lads exchanged shrugs, and went on past them to disappear up one of the walkways into the flats. Toby could even see which floor they went on to. If he'd had a pen and paper handy, he could have made a note of what they looked like, and where they'd gone.

Then he could have told the police, and he could have warned the old woman to take more care on pension days.

He looked down into the alley again, and it was empty. Everyone had gone home. Toby began to feel hungry. He looked down into the Wasteland, but the bullies had disappeared, too. It was getting dark.

He put the binoculars back into their case and hid them under the pile of blankets, just in case. Then he went back down the stairs, eased the wood from the window, and crept out into the dusk. His mum must be wondering what had kept him. He knew she'd scream at him if he said he'd been through the hoarding. He couldn't make up his mind what to tell her.

'You're late. What have you been up to?' said his mum, as soon as he put his nose through the door. 'Hurry up,' she said, without waiting for an answer. 'I'm signing you on at the doctor's straight away. Knowing you, you'll need him within the week. Yes, Nikki, you'd better come as well. Leave that telly alone! There's a time and place, isn't there? Come along, you two! I haven't got all night!'

They followed her down the stairs, turned right and went into the doctor's waiting-room. It was not exactly your purpose-built, easy to keep clean surgery. It was the front room of a shop, adapted. There was a waiting-room in front with a desk and some files for the recept-ionist-cum-nurse. At the back there was a loo and a treatment room and a small room for the doctor.

They got themselves signed on, and Kate said Toby had better stay and introduce himself to the doc while they were at it, but Nikki could go back if she would promise to get some jacket potatoes and put them into the microwave and no messing about with the controls, mind!

It was near closing time, so they didn't have very long to wait. Kate marched ahead of Toby into the doc's room, and said the usual about his having asthma and could she have a prescription, a repeat one, really, just to keep him going, and for emergencies.

Toby didn't get any further than the door. He gaped at the doctor.

'Yes?' said the doctor, giving Toby a half-smiling, half-frowning look. 'Something wrong?'

Toby wanted to say, 'Don't you know me?' because this was the man from his dream. There wasn't any difference that he could see. The doc was tall and thin and looked as if he never got enough sleep. He was wearing a white working coat over a guernsey sweater and jeans.

The jeans weren't right. The man in the dream hadn't worn jeans. He'd worn a pair of old army surplus trousers. But everything else was right, down to the long-fingered hands.

Only, the doc didn't seem to recognise Toby.

'Cat got your tongue?' said the doc, reaching for his stethoscope.

Toby shook his head. He let the doc examine him, and all the while he was thinking that this was the strangest thing that had ever happened to him. If it had been a dream, then why had the doc been in it?

The doc was talking to Kate in a polite sort of way, about her new job and the neighbourhood. Kate was going over the top as she usually did, saying what a disgrace this and that was, and why didn't the local people get into groups, organise themselves, get things moving.

Toby could see the doc didn't like that line of talk. It wasn't easy, he said.

'That's what they all say,' said Kate, lighting up a ciggie.

'Do you mind not smoking in here?' said the doc, still sounding tired, but this time also a bit annoyed.

'Oh, sorry,' said Kate, but she didn't sound sorry.

When she'd got the prescription for Toby she gave him a push towards the door. Toby hung back. He needed to say something to this man, but he couldn't think what. Then it came to him.

'Do you take a class in church on Sundays?' he asked.

'What?' said his mother, not at all amused, in fact a bit shocked.

'Well . . . no,' said the doc, looking properly at Toby for the first time, as a person, and not as a patient.

'Oh, sorry,' said Toby, feeling his whole body turn scarlet as a lobster.

'Well,' said the doc, 'I mean, our church isn't . . . you must have noticed what's happened to it. Do you go to church, then?'

'Of course not,' snapped Kate, giving Toby another push towards the door.

'Yes,' said Toby. 'At least, I did. I just thought, somehow, you might be interested. I know this church isn't . . . not now.'

'It's not been used as a church in my life-time,' said the doc, looking at Toby with something more than interest, just like the man in Toby's dream. Kate tried to twitch Toby towards the door once more, but Toby hadn't finished. He was amazed at himself, really, standing up to her and to him, too, a complete stranger. Only, the doc couldn't be a complete stranger if he'd been in the dream.

Kate said, through her teeth, 'Come along, Toby. The doctor's a busy man.'

'Not too busy for this,' said the doc, leaning forward and down to get close to Toby. The man in the dream had done that, too. 'Like you said, Mrs Webb, perhaps we have been letting things slide. Perhaps we ought to get together and do something about it.'

'I didn't mean about church,' said Kate.

'No,' said the doc, giving her an appraising look, 'I can see you didn't.'

Toby's heart beat faster and faster, and for a moment he thought he might be going into an asthma attack.

'Well,' he said, 'will you?'

'Will he do what?' demanded Kate. 'I don't know what's got into you, Toby Webb! You can't go around asking people to . . . well, I don't know what, exactly . . .'

'Yes,' said the doc, quickly.

'What?' she said, staring.

'Yes, if he can get some of his mates together and they're interested, then yes, I could come and take some sort of Sunday School class, I suppose.'

Her mouth fell open. Then her teeth clicked together with a snap. Her hand fell on Toby and propelled him out of the room with a You Wait! expression on her face. Toby turned round in the doorway and grinned back at the doc.

The doc grinned at Toby, too. He looked surprised at himself. Toby thought he'd probably regret what he'd promised to do. 'Probably,' thought Toby, 'the doc wouldn't have promised, if he hadn't got mad at Mum!' Toby grinned all the way back. When grown-ups fell out, kids didn't always lose by it.

# 4

'I'm bored!' said Nikki. It was a Saturday afternoon, it had been raining all day, and there was nothing to do except watch telly. There were old films and sports on, and she wasn't into them, either. Toby was way into the war film, but she turned the telly off, and after a moment he realised the sun was trying to come out, and it was kind of stuffy indoors.

He thought straight away about going to the church, to see what he could spot from the tower. He'd have to go carefully, though, because he was supposed to be looking after Nikki (that was a laugh!) while his mother was out. Also, the gang tended to go to the Wasteland, making a fire, drinking Coke, and generally messing around, any time they weren't actually in school.

Nikki tugged on a sweater and said, 'Come on! Show me the way into the churchyard.'

He tried to pretend he didn't know what she meant, but it was no good. It was never any good trying to pretend with her. She'd seen him looking at the bent bit of hoarding every time they'd gone past it. Being Nikki, she'd already wangled her way into a gang of girls and picked up most of the local gossip. She knew almost as much about the Wasteland as he did. Only, her friends didn't use the Wasteland for a meeting place. They went down the shopping centre instead, and hung around there. Nikki didn't think much of the shopping centre, and anyway, she knew she couldn't interest Toby in going there.

'So, come on!' she said, waiting for him at the bottom of their stairs. Toby locked up and showed her the way into the Wasteland, first looking round to see that the gang weren't there. They weren't, luckily. He showed her around, wondering all the time if he could tell her about the dream, but deciding against it in the end. After all, who would believe, when looking at that mess, that there could ever be a garden there?

He told her about the doc, though. She thought that was hysterical. She'd only been to church once in her life, and that was once too much, she said. A christening, or something. Babies screaming their heads off, and mothers being cross and tired and a man in a stupid outfit trying to talk over the noise. Catch her going again! she said.

Toby surprised himself, and her. 'I'd like it, though. And the doc promised to come and talk to us. He said if we could get some of our friends together . . .'

'You ain't got no friends over here!'

That was true. Toby was silent. Perhaps the doc had counted on that. Perhaps the doc really would be glad of an 'out'. Kate wouldn't help, he knew that. His mum didn't reckon much to the doc, muttering on about old-fashioned and interfering and 'Who did he think he was, anyway!'

He was staring at nothing much when he heard the gang in the street, banging their way along the outside of the hoarding.

'Quick!' Toby grabbed Nikki and drew her into the corner where the low window was. He worked the board loose, pushed her inside despite her shriek of protest, and followed. Fitting the window back over the frame, he hissed at her to keep quiet, and he'd show her a secret.

He led the way up and into the church. The sun was coming through a high window, slatted with boards, but still letting in the light. The floor was barred with strokes of light and dark.

Nikki hop-scotched across them, waving her arms.

Toby hugged himself. Why was the church so cold? And why didn't Nikki feel it? His mum said Toby took after his dad. He wished he'd got a picture of his dad, but his mum wasn't one for keeping junk around the place. She said he'd been quite a looker in his day, but Toby couldn't imagine it, somehow.

'Is this all there is?' said Nikki.

He led her through the door in the panelling, and up and up, until they reached the Lookout. That's what Toby called it in his mind; the Lookout. He showed her the view from all four windows, and then he showed her the binoculars and told her about the old woman and the two lads whom he'd been pretty sure had intended to rob her.

'You should have written it down, Hawkeye, and gone to the police!' said Nikki, trying out the glasses herself.

Toby had thought much the same himself. 'No pencil. No paper.'

'What about this?' She picked up the notebook and glanced through it. 'There are some blank pages at the end. You look, and I'll write.'

She fished a ballpoint from the debris in her pocket and wrote in large letters:

NICOLA JANE WEBB,
27 PARADISE ROW,
HACKNEY, LONDON,
THE WORLD,
THE UNIVERSE.

'It's not yours,' said Toby, rather too late to do any good.

'It is now,' she said. 'What can you see?'

He focussed the glasses on the alley, but there was no-one there. The walkways were fairly busy, but there was no sign of the bad lads. There were some old men sunning themselves on a bench by the bus-stop and at the far end of the school he could see a game of football going on.

There was a lot of shouting down in the Wasteland. Nikki tried to open a window, but couldn't. Toby found out how to work the catch, so that one of the panes tilted out and up. The voices increased in strength.

'He did! They should have called the police!'

'He didn't do it! He never! He wouldn't! You're a rotten liar!'

'It's you who's lying. Everyone knows he got the push for stealing . . .'

'It was a fit-up! He never took anything, not a brick, not a plank . . .'

'Who're you kidding, Red? Old Man Wittem wouldn't have pushed your dad out, not after all those years, if he hadn't been certain for sure!'

'It was a fit-up, I tell you! One day everyone will know and then they'll be sorry, and . . .'

'Tell us another! Everyone knows he was sneaking things out the back way at weekends, and selling them off cheap to Gregors . . .'

'You're a rotten liar!'

'Who're you shoving! Shove him back!'

There was a confused babble of sounds and several thumps. Toby and Nikki tried and tried to see what was happening, but the ruckus was so close to the tower that they couldn't see much of anything, except arms and legs whirling about.

Finally the group moved off, leaving the carroty lad they'd call 'Red' rubbing various parts of his anatomy, and swearing to himself. He kicked everything in sight, and sat down with his head in his hands.

Toby and Nikki looked down at him in silence. They couldn't get out with Red sitting there.

Toby picked up the glasses and scanned the streets below. The name Old Man Wittem rang a bell. Yes, there it was. Builders' Merchants, A.M.Wittem and

Sons, Est. 1956. There was a big double shop front on the street, and at the back there was a crowded yard which stretched back and back, and went out through double gates onto the street which ran parallel to the shop front. There was no sign of anyone in the shop now. It had closed for the weekend. But in the yard there were some men loading things on to a lorry.

'Funny peculiar,' said Toby, watching the men. 'They've closed the gates on to the road, and they keep looking around, and stopping to listen. Are they afraid of someone catching them at work on a Saturday afternoon?'

There were two men, one large and stout, the other thin with long hair under a checked cap. One of them opened the gates on to the street, looked both ways, and signalled to his mate, who drove the lorry out and round the corner.

'Making a delivery,' said Nikki, not particularly interested. 'Overtime rates. Is that Wittem and Spittem, then? Is that where Red's dad used to work?'

'Most funny peculiar,' said Toby. 'They've stopped by another lorry, in that dark cul-de-sac, see? Tail to tail, and they're transferring all the stuff from the first lorry on to the second. The first lorry is a Wittem lorry. It's got it painted on the side. The second lorry is . . . can't see. Something Gregor.'

Nikki screeched with excitement. 'It's the thieves! It's them! We've caught them in the act! Let me see!' She tried to grab the glasses but Toby stuck to them.

'We'll lose them! Get writing, quick!'

'Where's my pen? Oh, on the floor. Right. How do you spell McGregor?'

'I think I can read the licence number.' He gave it to her, and then described the two men involved.

'Is one of them Red's dad?'

'Who knows what Red's dad looks like?'

The Wittem lorry drove back into the Wittem yard,

the two men came out and locked the double gates behind them. The McGregor lorry drove off eastwards.

Nikki said, 'What do we do now? Go to the police? Or tell Red?'

'If we tell Red, he'll have to know about this place, and it won't be a secret any more.'

'We don't have to tell him how we know. We could sort of drop hints.'

Toby wished they could, but no-one would believe them, if they didn't know how they'd come by their information. It was very hard. This place really had been a sort of sanctuary in the Land of the Baddies. But. . .

'No, we'll have to tell them,' said Toby. 'We can't let them get away with it.'

Nikki pulled a face but followed him down the stairs and out through the escape hatch.

# 5

'Hey, where you come from?' said Red, startled by their popping up out of the ground almost at his feet. Not only was his hair a violent red, but he had so many freckles, he looked as if someone had emptied a pepper-pot over his skin. Red looked as if he'd been crying, maybe. Toby could see that Nikki was going to ask him about that, so hurried to speak first.

'What's your dad look like? Is he a thinnish chap with long hair?'

Red just gaped.

'Has he got a checked cap? Or is he big and stout with lots of bushy hair?'

Nikki hopped from one leg to the other. 'Tell him! We saw them, we did! From up the top! Clear as clear! Loading stuff on to one lorry, and then taking it round the back to put it on a 'Gregor's lorry. You got to tell your dad and the police'll catch the men and everything will be all right again!'

Red went on gaping at them, his eyes almost dropping out.

'Up there,' said Toby, trying to be patient and pointing up at the tower. 'You can see for miles. You can see into all the back yards. Everything. We got the licence number and all.'

Red shot into the air and made for the hoarding door. A couple of the gang were hanging around outside, and he screeched at them, 'Told you so! It weren't me dad! I'm going to fetch him . . .!'

Toby and Nikki hesitated at the exit. More members of the gang were coming up all the time and it was going to be difficult, if not impossible, to push through them.

'What's all this, then?' said the tallest boy, who was always called 'Skinny'. 'What you two been up to?'

'Up inside the church,' said Nikki, proudly. 'Toby found the lookout, and we spied on the thieves and got them, so there!'

'You can't get inside,' said Skinny. 'We know. We tried.'

'They're lying!' said another of the gang, shoving Toby along.

'Just hang about,' said Toby, patiently. 'We'll show you, but we've got to wait till Red's dad comes, or they won't know the way.'

'You'd better show us now!'

'No, Toby's right!' said Nikki, hopping from one foot to the other. 'We've got to wait!'

'We don't wait for anyone!' said Skinny, but he didn't do any shoving, and he was a bit half-hearted about it, so they left Toby alone. He couldn't get away, of course. They'd be watching for that. If he tried it, they'd jump him. He could feel that they'd like to jump him. Even with Nikki there.

Toby felt in his pockets for his inhaler, but he hadn't got it with him. In a moment he'd begin to wheeze, and they'd realise how frightened he was of them, and then they'd jump him for sure.

Red came sprinting back along the pavement, with a large ginger-haired man in tow. They only lived round the corner, and Mr Red had been sitting watching telly, not expecting anything to happen.

Mr Red was even larger than the man who'd been loading the lorry, and he was so angry he looked like you'd get an electric shock if you touched him.

'Well?' he said. 'Who saw what?'

Toby told him. Nikki produced the book, and showed where she'd written down the licence numbers and the descriptions of the people who'd been moving the stuff.

Mr Red bellowed, 'That's the Something Something foreman! He's been picking on me and now I see why! Right, young man! You're coming with me to the police, and we'll get this sorted!'

It wasn't possible to keep it from their mum. In one way Toby didn't want to, and in another way he did. His mum had a habit of moving into situations and taking them over. She'd already got the neighbourhood plastered with posters advertising meetings for this and protests for that. You couldn't overlook someone like that, but it didn't make for a nice quiet life with her around.

Toby was all for a nice, quiet life. His ideal would be to have just one good friend, like in the old days. To go to a youth club once a week, maybe. To read and think and talk everything over with his one friend. Not to get into hassles, because they started off his asthma.

Trouble was for people like Nikki and his mum, who thrived on it. Nikki really enjoyed the drama of having the police around, showing everyone how they'd got into the church and what they could see from the Lookout. Toby would have melted away and let them get on with it, but they seemed to think they couldn't prove anything without him to go over and over it. He was stuck with it.

On the way to school on Monday, Toby found Red waiting for him at the corner. Red walked all the way to school with him, stuck to him at playtime, and introduced him properly to all the gang. Red couldn't keep his mouth shut about what had been happening. Soon everyone in the neighbourhood knew. The police acted on 'information supplied', and traced the real thieves. The foreman got the sack and Red's dad was made foreman in his place.

All Toby wanted to do was to forget the whole thing and get on with his life, but they wouldn't let him.

Skinny and Red and Fats and the rest of the gang seemed to assume he'd be happy to join up with them and no hard feelings about what had gone on before.

It was all right, Toby thought. Not ideal, but all right. Except one day the doc stopped them all in the street as they came home from school one afternoon.

The doc was hopping out of his car with his bag, looking harassed as usual, when he spotted Toby at the edge of the group.

'Hi!' said the doc, just as he had in the dream. 'So you got your mates organised, did you? I heard you'd got into the church. Will half ten this Sunday be all right?'

Toby flooded scarlet all over. 'I dunno. I'd sort of forgotten . . .'

'Well, are they your mates, or aren't they?' said the doc, looking at his watch, and then at Skinny and Red. 'Hi, Skinny. Is your mum feeling better on those pills? Hi, Red. Glad to hear about your dad getting his job back. Half ten, right?'

'Sure,' said Red, grinning. 'Whatever you say, doc.'

'Got something on, have we?' said Skinny to Toby. 'You weren't going to keep us out, were you?'

Toby took a deep breath, holding off the asthma feeling. 'I didn't think you'd be interested. It was sort of private.'

'Sunday morning? Why not?' said Skinny. 'We're bored out of our skulls, Sundays. And if it's something to do with the doc, it'll be all right.'

'Sure. You're on,' said some of the others, crowding around.

'It's stories,' said Toby, desperately. 'Making sense of life.'

'Go on,' said Skinny, still interested.

'Church,' said Toby, turkey-cock red and hating this. 'Jesus.'

'Jesus?' said Skinny. He looked astounded, and so did

everyone else. But no-one laughed.

'Yes,' said Toby, wondering where his inhaler was. He'd left it at home, he felt sure. 'Jesus stories. Telling us why he came to us, what he did, and what he said. It's all about following him, the best way to live. The only way to live. It makes sense of everything.'

'About "the World, the Universe, Everything"?' said someone at the back.

''Srubbish!' said somebody else, but he didn't say it too loud.

Skinny said, 'You mean the doc would take time out to talk to us about it? Would he? Grownups don't usually. They think we're stupid, wouldn't understand. Or they just don't care.'

'You mean it would be about God, all of it?' said Red, doubtfully.

'Yes,' said Toby, letting out a long, wheezy breath. It was probably the bravest thing he'd ever done, to say it like that, in front of them all.

There was a broody sort of silence.

'OK, I'm on,' said Red, hunching his shoulders as if expecting to get hit again. 'I owe you one, I suppose.'

All eyes transferred to Red, who blushed but didn't flinch.

'OK,' said Skinny. 'Let's give it a whirl, shall we? The doc's an OK sort and if we don't like it, we don't have to go again, do we?'

Some of the gang shrugged and agreed. Some shrugged and went off without saying whether they'd come or not.

Toby felt he'd rather like to sit down. Talk about tension! He slipped through the hoarding and sat down on a convenient lump of masonry. The Wasteland looked as bad as ever. The flats loomed as dark as ever.

But the sky was blue-blue, and the gilded weathervane winked and twirled in the breeze.

'Hi,' the man had said. 'You come to help?'

Toby felt he was beginning to understand what the dream meant.

Their mum was in a right state. She'd organised meetings and she'd papered the place with leaflets, wearing out her best pair of boots walking the streets, and hardly anyone had turned up to listen to her. When her meetings failed, she'd knocked on doors, and she'd met with the same response. Zilch.

She was so angry her voice had faded out on her.

She was angry with the twins, too. She didn't mind their helping the police, much. It was stupid, of course, to get mixed up in such things, and even more stupid to make friends with the gang, even though she supposed the twins knew it was bad housing and bad social conditions which had made the gang what they were. But she was livid that they'd disobeyed her and gone into the Wasteland and even more livid when she heard how they'd broken into the church.

She lectured them this way and that till they were sick of the sound of the word 'church'. And when the doc stopped her in the street and told her he'd got hold of the old keys to the church door, so's they could use it on Sunday, she just gaped!

When Nikki had first heard about the projected Sunday meeting, she'd said they could count her out. Sundays were not for going to church, stupid that! Sundays were for making up a foursome to go swimming or something. Something active.

When Nikki realised her mum was dead against it, she changed her mind. 'I'll come, maybe,' she said. 'But only if you swear you won't laugh, or tell on me to my friends. Right?'

'Right,' said Toby. Toby wasn't too happy about the way things were going. He felt as if he'd stepped on to a roller-coaster, and it was getting out of control.

One afternoon when the gang stopped off at the Wasteland to have a quick fag and a natter, they found the door into the side of the church wide open, and a cloud of dust coming out. They crowded in to see what was happening, and found the doc and his receptionist and a strange gent in a beaten-up but originally good suit, all trying to clean the place out. The gent in the good suit looked as if he'd got a lemon slice in his mouth, it turned down so much at the corners. Then he smiled at them and his mouth turned up and up into a Cheshire Cat grin. You could see then that he was really an OK type, after all.

It turned out he was the churchwarden, or had been years ago when the church had been a church. He'd had charge of the keys all this time, and had volunteered to help doc get everything ready for Sunday.

Most of the gang agreed to help, and got down to it, but Toby retreated from the dust clouds, taking Red and Skinny up the tower with him. They sat on the bed and pretended they weren't feeling excited about what was happening.

Red said, lighting up a fag, 'Did I tell you me dad's been made foreman?'

He had, several times a day for the last week.

Skinny said, 'It's still going to be a dump, downstairs. Couldn't we meet somewheres else?'

'No, I don't think so,' said Toby. 'It's a church, see.'

'Not much of a church. Not how I remember churches. We used to go to the one over the far side of the shopping centre, from the first school. Nice, in a way. If you liked that sort of thing. Carols and that. Harvest. Boring, though.'

'This is still a church,' said Toby, 'even now.'

'How? It's just an empty space.'

'Yes,' said Toby. 'I think that's the point. Like the Wasteland. We could make it into a garden, if we liked. Or dump rubbish on it. Same as life. Our lives. We can tackle the bad bits in ourselves and encourage the good.

We can make ourselves grow towards the light, or we can let ourselves be overtaken by junk, and pests, and all manner of creepy-crawlies . . .'

'Good and evil, eh?' said Red. 'Well, I'm all for fighting off the baddies, if that's what you mean.'

'All this is Jesus talk, I suppose,' said Skinny. 'It's too deep for me.'

Now Skinny wasn't stupid, and Toby knew that, but he also knew that getting to know Jesus made you face up to problems in your own life, which you could duck if you liked, but you'd never feel good with yourself, after. He was still facing up to them, himself. He couldn't help Skinny. Or Red. Or anyone. He was still struggling, even if he did get occasional moments of certainty. Of love. Every now and then he was dead sure Jesus loved him and was with him. And then it would go.

Red finished his fag, and they went back down to help.

# 6

Their mum did her nutcake on Sunday morning.

'We need a church here like we need a hole in the head,' she said, slamming bread into the toaster, and punching it down. 'What good did a church ever do, tell me that! What we need here is action! We need people to get out and get working on something real, something that would really do some good!'

Toby chewed on his muesli, thinking that 'good' had to start somewhere, that it had to come from loving God, and that then it went through you and out into the world. Sort of. But you needed help. Stoking up. Filling up, like at a petrol filling station. The church was his petrol filling station.

'. . .and another thing! That doctor friend of yours, he's just typical of the attitude they've got around here. They say, Yes, it's all wrong about the bad housing and the damp and the high rents, but it's none of our business. Or they say, Yes, but what can we do about it? They don't Think! They don't get off their backsides and Act! That's what that doctor of yours ought to be doing! He ought to be helping me get Something Done, instead of wasting time with prayers and preaching and singing hymns!'

'There aren't going to be prayers and preaching, are there?' said Nikki, horrified. 'I mean, boring!'

'I don't know what he's going to do,' said Toby. 'All I know is, it'll be good. Everyone says the doc is an OK type.'

'Not in my book, he isn't!' said Mum, catching the toast in mid-air as it shot out of the toaster. Toby and

41

Nikki watched in admiration. No-one but their mum could make the toaster work, or catch the toast as it flew out. She was something else, their mum!

Ten o'clock, and they were on their way.

'How many's coming?' said Nikki, looking over her shoulder as if wishing she'd gone swimming instead.

'Dunno. Red and Skinny for sure. I think.'

They stopped to admire a new slogan on one of the hoardings òutside the church. Someone had taken a spray can to it. A real artist, that.

"Sunday. Half ten. Come and get it!"

'Fats did that,' said Nikki full of admiration.

'Fats?' Toby couldn't remember who Fats was, and then he did. Fats was a large, slow-moving black boy on the fringe of the gang.

'He does all the spraying around here. Two colours, sometimes. I think he's brill.'

They didn't sneak in through the hoarding, but went round to the front door of the church. One whole section of hoarding had been removed, giving access to the steps which led up to the main door under the tower. The doors were standing open. No-one was going in, except them.

Inside it was wide and high and empty.

The doc was there, unstacking a lot of chairs.

'Hi,' he said. 'Do you know how many's coming? I brought these from my waiting room, and there's the three old pews, not bad, still usable.'

'Maybe it's just us three,' said Toby. 'Maybe Red and Skinny, but I'm not even sure about them.'

'That's OK. Jesus said that where two or more were met together in his name, he'd be with them. So we've got a head start.'

'You don't need me, then,' said Nikki. But she grinned, and helped him range the chairs in a double semi-circle. There was a lot of puffing and grunting, and down the stairs from the Lookout came Skinny and the church-warden, carrying the rolled-up rug which had been on the floor there. They took it out into the Wasteland and banged some of the dust out of it before laying it in front of the chairs in the middle of the floor.

'No altar,' said the doc sadly. 'That all went, in the blitz. The bells went, too. I remember my grandfather telling me there were two bells called Peter and Paul, and he used to ring them, every Sunday.'

Red sauntered in, whistling, with his hands in his pockets, as if he were having a stroll down to the shops. He stopped whistling, and threw himself down into a chair. He put his feet up on another chair and leaned back. Toby looked at Red, kind of agitated, not knowing what to say about the feet on the chair, but feeling it wasn't right to behave like that.

There was a stir in the porch and in sailed a West Indian woman, large and smiling, wearing a hat and white gloves and carrying a hymn book! Behind her, looking awkward and shiny, came Fats, and five more clones of Fats, each one decreasing in size.

Mrs Fats shook hands with the doc and said, 'We are so glad you are opening up this church again. It's quite a job getting the family to the church on the other side of the shopping centre.'

She plopped herself down in the front row, and looked at Red, who took his feet off his chair, and sat upright. Fats made as if to join Red and Skinny at the back, but his mum gave him a look, so he sat down with her and his brothers in the front.

The churchwarden wandered to the porch, holding his pocket watch in his hand, and in trooped every single member of the gang, all talking loudly to show they weren't doing anything out of the ordinary. They got themselves seated and then changed their positions, and changed again. By which time Mr Red had arrived, with his wife and a girl about Nikki's age. Also a couple of Nikki's friends from school.

Then there was a pause. From a distant church came the sound of a clock chiming the half hour.

'We should start, I think,' said the doc. He'd set a chair for himself, but stood behind it, holding on to it. There was an awkward silence, while no-one but Mrs Fats seemed to know what to do. She bent her head and seemed to be praying, so everyone – or more or less everyone – copied her.

Then she sat up and looked at the doc, and he said, 'I'm not a minister. You all know that. I'm only here because some of the kids asked me to come and tell them about God and what he means to me. I didn't expect to see so many people here . . .'

Three more lads slipped in around the back and went to sit on the far side, out of the sunlight. They were followed by a single old woman, and after her, another two young married women, one holding a toddler in her arms.

'. . .but I can tell you that if it weren't for the love of God, I wouldn't be here. He's part of my life. I know some of you have God in your lives, too. Some of you can probably tell the kids more about him than I can, but they asked me first, so I'll make a start and perhaps that's all I'm going to be needed for. Just to make a start, and then for someone else to take over.'

He was nervous. He unclutched himself from the chair and looked around, blindly.

Toby thought, He's forgotten his lines. He needs a prompt.

People were still drifting in. All the chairs were full, and the pews, and one or two people were standing at the back, propping themselves up against the walls.

The doc said, 'The kids wanted a story, one that made sense of everything. I thought of lots of stories, but if you wanted just one, then this is it.

' "Once, not so long ago in Africa, every boy had to undergo a night out in the wild before he was allowed to join the tribe as an adult. It was pretty frightening out there in the wild. There were lions and hyenas. Some of the lads believed there were even worse things; evil spirits waiting to grab you, and drag you away. But you had to go through with it. Everyone did.

' "Now there was this boy, a nice lad, brave enough in the daytime but there were lots of things about the night which scared him. He knew he had to go through with it, and he didn't know how he was going to manage it. His father taught him how to outface the wild animals, and how to conquer his fears. His father showed him how to light a fire, and to keep it burning all the night long. That way, no harm would come to the boy. But he must keep watch, he must keep feeding the fire, he must not let it die down.

' "The time came for the boy's trial, and his father took him out into the wilderness. The boy was afraid. He knew his father could not help him any more. The boy gathered wood for the fire, and set it alight, and in the dusk his father walked away, leaving his son alone to face the night.

' "At first the night was as bad as the boy had feared. He fancied that every bush hid a lion, or some other creature on the prowl. But he fed the fire, and he kept watch by it, and gradually he came to realise that his father had spoken the truth, and that the fire did keep the evil things of the night at a distance. It seemed a very long night to the boy, but at length there was a lightening of the sky. The trees, the bushes, became silhouetted as the dawn approached.

' "One shape remained the same. Someone – a man – was standing not far off, had been standing there all night, watching over the boy. In the new light of the morning sun, the boy recognised his father's figure. His father had stood by him all that while, watching. Waiting. Loving him." '

No one spoke.

No one could speak.

Mrs Fats stood up and spread her magnificent arms high and wide.

'Allelujah!' she cried.

Everyone looked at her with open mouths.

Toby had never heard anyone say 'Allelujah!' like that before. It was one of the most astonishing things that had ever happened to him.

Everyone unstuck their eyes from Mrs Fats and looked at the doc.

He said, 'Er, should we discuss that story, or was it clear?'

Mrs Fats said, 'Clear as daylight. God is our Father and watches over us throughout life.'

'The Bible is his word, and our guide as to how we should live,' said the churchwarden, with his Cheshire Cat grin.

Skinny said, 'Yes, but what about the fire?' And then turned red at making himself conspicuous.

'Well,' said the doc, 'The fire is our effort to follow his teaching. What we put into life. I put in my skill as a doctor. But it can be almost anything, don't you think, so long as it is done with love for God?'

'You mean schoolwork can be done for God?' said Skinny, not believing it for a minute.

'Oh, yes it can,' said the doc. 'If you love Jesus with all your heart, and all your mind, and all your strength, then his love will shine through everything you do. This is the time of your life when you learn about building and lighting and feeding a fire. That's the skill side of it, but there is another side, and that's spreading the Good News. That's another way of feeding the fire. Like the boy who spoke up for God. The boy who started all this. He lit a fire, too, didn't he?'

Toby gaped. Did the doc mean him? Was what he'd done so important? A lot of the gang were looking at him and nodding, thoughtful-like, not taking the mick.

Skinny said, 'I get it. You mean, we got to keep feeding the fire by keeping the church going?'

'The church is you. Or rather, you are the church.'

'What, me? But a church is a building.'

'The church is the people and what they do.'

Skinny didn't get that, and Toby wasn't sure he had, either. Mr Red cleared his throat. 'But you'll open up the church again.' He made it a statement and not a question.

'I don't know,' said the doc. 'It's not my decision to make. You'll have to ask the proper authorities.'

The churchwarden checked his watch again. 'This is not a formal service but as we are gathered here together in the name of God, he knows we're here, and he knows our needs and everything that's in our hearts. Maybe he'll make it clear what he wants us to do, if we pray about it now, in silence, and if we go on praying through the week. I have permission to open the church on Sunday mornings for an informal prayer meeting, so I suggest we come together again, at the same time, next week.'

Everyone bent their heads and stared at the floor. Perhaps some of them prayed. Toby felt so muddled and stirred up that he couldn't concentrate, and he was glad when people around him began to shift back in their chairs and stare around.

Some people got up. Mrs Fats said, 'Where's the collection plate?'

There wasn't one, but everyone dropped some money onto the doc's chair on their way out.

The place was almost empty when Kate came out from where she'd been leaning in the porch, keeping out of sight, but able to hear everything. She looked at the doc, and he looked at her.

He said, 'The flame can be someone trying to get better housing conditions for people who can't help themselves, if it's done for the love of God and their fellow men. I'm sorry I didn't help you before. I'll put one of your posters up in the waiting room, if you like.'

She nodded. She looked kind of melted, as if she didn't know what expression to wear. Toby could have sworn she dropped some money on the chair on her way out, but maybe he imagined it.

# 7

The weather changed overnight. The golden ship on top of the tower creaked and heaved as wind and rain beat first from this quarter and then from that. It wasn't only the weather that took a turn for the worse. There was a spate of muggings in the area, mostly in the alleys and walkways leading to the flats, but also in the narrow old streets around.

There was some nasty bullying in the school playground, and though Toby was pretty sure that his lot were not involved, it left a bad taste. Everything seemed dirtier than usual. The streets didn't seem to look clean even after the council men had been round. Graffiti was sprayed over everything in sight, and most of it was directed against 'The Holy Ones'. Anyone who'd been at the church that Sunday was automatically 'A Holy'. It wasn't nice.

Toby felt desperate about it. Sometimes he got fanciful ideas into his head – his mum said it came from reading too much fiction – and now it seemed to him that the doc had held up a shining mirror to the evil that existed in the Paradise Estate. The evil things that lived there didn't like being shown up like that, and were reacting, striking back at everything that was good and clean.

He didn't know what to do about it. He thought everything would be all right when they'd had another meeting in the church, but suddenly everyone seemed doubtful about going again. Nikki was the first to defect, announcing that she and her friends didn't reckon much on church, and would be going swimming as usual the following Sunday.

Then their mum came up to the top floor, and banged around, checking on window catches and squeaky floorboards, making lists of things that needed attention. Toby was lying on his bed, trying to do his geography, but she didn't go, even after she'd touched everything in sight.

She said, 'I didn't know you were a secret Christian.' She seemed both angry and amused about it.

'Not secret. Just new to it.'

'You're not serious!' Now she was more angry than amused.

'Yes, probably.'

'There's nothing there, you know. There is no God.'

She sat on his bed and flicked out her ciggies. He hated her to smoke in his room, but he didn't like to say so. He wriggled a bit in protest, but said nothing.

'Well, cat got your tongue again?' she said.

He didn't want to argue, not with his mum, so he said nothing at all. The funny thing was that what she'd said didn't worry him. He knew God existed, because he'd felt God's love around him.

She flicked open the Bible at his bedside. 'What's that? Your father's, I suppose. Yes, it would be. You take after him in so many ways. I might have guessed.'

'Was he a Christian, too?'

She stubbed out her fag, and got up, making a face and saying something about getting the supper ready. She went out without answering his question, but Toby didn't really need to have it answered. He knew. His dad's Bible had been very thoroughly read, and special passages had been marked with a heavy line in a soft pencil. It gave Toby a good feeling to track down these passages and think about them, remembering that his dad had liked them.

He remembered what the churchwarden had said, about praying for guidance about the church. Toby wished he knew how to pray properly. Somehow it wasn't right to say, Please may I have a personal stereo for my birthday, and in the same breath say, Please may I have a church. He could feel there was a lot of difference between those two prayers. God must know they needed a church on the Paradise Estate. He didn't need telling.

Kate started seeing a smarmy sort of councillor chap, someone high up on one of her committees. He smiled like a shark, thought Toby, who'd disliked him on sight. Toby thought the feeling was probably mutual, because 'Dear Jeff' talked across Toby rather than to him, whenever he called at the flat.

Part of the hoarding around the church site blew down, so that everyone could see how awful the Wasteland was. Kate went and saw someone at the Council about the Wasteland, which she thought she could get cleaned up, and maybe use as an Adventure Playground in the summer holidays.

Lots of people thought that was a good idea, maybe the best idea she'd had yet. They went round saying they hadn't been at all sure about appointing a woman as Youth and Community Worker, but maybe the council had known what they were doing, after all. Nikki and most of the gang thought it was a good idea, too.

Toby didn't know why he didn't think it was a good idea. It was something to do with the dream, maybe. That bit of land was a garden. No, wrong. It *could* be a garden, but it ought to be a garden for everyone. It was all wrong to think of tarmac on the ground, and no roses.

He tried to see their point of view. There wasn't a park for miles around, not a proper one. You had to get on the Tube and go out to Greenwich before you saw anything much in the way of greenery. They were pulling down some of the small old streets and building expensive housing estates, but those places wouldn't be like Paradise Row. They would be for stockbrokers and money men, and there'd probably be gates at the entrances of the new estates, to keep ordinary kids from straying in and playing on their nicely kept greens.

Everything hinged on Sunday, thought Toby. Sunday would make everything come right.

Sunday was a disaster. It couldn't have been worse. It rained, and it blew, and though some people turned up at the right time at church, there weren't nearly as many as before. Mrs Fats didn't come, and nor did any of her family. The gang showed up, but seeing how things were, they went away again.

The doc let them down. He didn't turn up. Not at all.

The churchwarden got up and read them a piece from the Bible, and said they should sing a hymn. Only they hadn't anyone to lead the singing, and no piano, not even a guitar, so that was a flop. Then the churchwarden prayed aloud a bit, and everyone bowed their heads and listened, but it was all old-fashioned words and not much of it went into Toby's head. Nor into anyone else's, either, he thought. The churchwarden asked if anyone else would like to pray, but they kept their faces blank and sat on their hands.

It was horribly embarrassing. Toby wanted to die, it was so ghastly.

He knew in his head that God must be there, because there were ten of them in the church, but he couldn't feel it.

After lunch he went into the Wasteland and sat on a broken-down wall. He was too miserable to talk to anyone. He was even a bit annoyed when Fats came in and sat beside him. It had stopped raining, and they were in a sheltered corner.

Suddenly the doc came striding over to join them. He looked upset.

The two boys looked at him, and he looked at them. He sat down and put his head in his hands.

'Didn't they tell you? Didn't you get my message? I

did send. I didn't want to let you down. But I couldn't get away. I had to get her into hospital, and get the kid looked after. You didn't hear what happened? Poor Mrs Rogers. You remember her? She came to church last week. Her husband left her nine weeks ago, and she's been scraping along, waiting for the DHSS to sort out her money, and finally her giro came through and she went around paying everyone what they'd lent her, and the shops. She was over the moon! I saw her in passing yesterday, and she waved to me, and called out everything was coming up roses. They mugged her this morning, two of them, right at her front door with the child looking on and screaming. They took the rest of her money, ransacked her flat. Took her wedding ring, even. No one went to help. They daren't. I suppose some people must know who's doing it, but they won't say. Too scared. It was only when the child went on screaming and screaming that someone dared look out and saw. Well, maybe she'll be all right. Maybe. It's a Sunday. Not much doing at the hospital. I couldn't leave her till they'd found someone to admit her. Concussion, you know, and stitches needed. Poor woman, I thought of you all, waiting. I knew how important it was.'

'It was a disaster,' said Toby.

'Me mum made us go back to our old church,' said Fats. 'She said that was our church, and she was a member there, and committed to it. I didn't want to go. I wanted to come here, but when me mum tells you, you stay told.'

The doc looked at the church. He hadn't shaved that day. It should have been his day off.

Toby wanted to comfort him, but didn't know how.

'What I think is,' said Fats, 'that you are a doctor first and have to put that first, all the time.'

'Yes,' said the doc. 'That's what I kept telling myself. But it didn't make me feel any better.' He looked vaguely around. 'What a mess this place is. Everything is. Sorry, boys.'

Toby said, 'Can I tell you something? The night I came here, I had this dream. You were in it. At least, I suppose it wasn't you, but that I must have seen you without realising it, the day we arrived. You were here, about where you're sitting now, and there were flowers coming up all over, and roses. You were tying roses up to a trellis that went all up that wall over there, the wall of your surgery, with our flat above. I helped you. We talked, but I can't remember much about it, except you asked if I'd come to help you.'

'Help me do what?'

'I can't remember, exactly. I think it was about choosing between good and evil, and not letting evil strangle you; like weeds in a garden. There was something about the church, too, about needing it in your life.'

'That's lovely, Toby,' said the doc, really smiling. He looked a lot younger and less tired when he smiled like that. He said, 'Well, boys, I'm glad I saw you. Any time, really, I mean it. Any time. If you need me, I'll be there. I've got a bleeper. My receptionist can call me and I'll hear it, wherever I am.'

'But you're not on twenty-four hour call,' said Fats. 'You've got to rest sometime.'

The doc began to laugh. 'I've just thought. God's never tired. He doesn't have to take a rest, or have a day off. He's on twenty-four hour call. If you want him, you just give him a bell, right?'

The doc stood up, and looked around. 'Come to think of it, there are three of us here, and I think we met to talk about him, so he is here, and maybe he put that into my mind, about God being on twenty-four hour call. Perhaps I needed reminding about it, too.'

'If he is here,' said Toby, hesitating to ask for more, 'and of course you're right, and he is here, then could you tell us how to pray? I mean, I know about shopping

54

lists of things I want, but it's not the same, now. I mean, what I want now . . . it's different. But I don't know the words.'

'Use your own words, Toby. Just speak from the heart. I do.' The doc put his hand on Toby's shoulder. Toby could feel the weight of the doc's hand, warm through his T-shirt. The contact steadied Toby.

The doc bent his head. 'Lord, you know we met to be with you. You know the troubles that surround us. You know how tired and discouraged we are. It seemed as if opening up the old church would solve all our problems, but we are not sure . . . perhaps we are too weak . . . perhaps we are not the right people. Guide us. Help us to do what you want us to do. Strengthen and comfort us. In the name of Jesus. Amen.'

'Amen,' said Fats.

'Amen,' whispered Toby.

The doc stood there for a moment, still with his hand on Toby's shoulder. Then the doc put his other hand on Fats' shoulder, and left it there a while. Toby looked up and smiled at the doc. Fats looked up and smiled, too. The doc smiled back down at them.

Fats said, 'That was one of the best church services I've ever been to.'

Toby looked back at the tower, and then he looked up at the doc. 'Is that what you meant by saying that we, us people, are the church?'

The doc nodded. 'Thanks, lads. See you next Sunday, if not before.'

'What a dump!' said Kate, looking angry. She was showing the Wasteland to her new friend Jeff, and he was nodding, and agreeing with everything she said. Toby and Nikki hung around, being polite, and trying not to get in the way. Both Kate and Jeff tended to walk into people when they got het up, and most of the time they seemed to be in a state about something. This time it was about the Wasteland and the church.

'Honestly, you'd think they'd have done something about it by now,' said Kate. 'The council said they couldn't do anything because it didn't belong to them, and they couldn't even clean it up if we did get permission to use the land. The church people said would I write in and they'd consider it at their next Diocesan meeting, which might be in a year's time for all I know. The church people won't sell to the council, and the council won't put a compulsory purchase order on the site because they don't want a hassle with the Church Commissioners and anyway they say they haven't any money for frills! Frills!'

She snorted, and Jeff nodded his heavy, bearded head in agreement.

'You tried!' he said.

'I could weep!' she said. 'They say there's a crypt under the church, and it goes right under the Wasteland, apparently, hardly damaged at all by the bomb. They patched it up immediately after, and they assure me the whole crypt is watertight. One big hall, and several smaller rooms. If we could only get hold of that, think what we could make of it! A proper Community Centre, instead of that old shack down the other end of the shops which is probably going to get pulled down any day now, anyway. We could run a Luncheon Club for pensioners here, and a Toddlers group, and maybe a small nursery, or a creche. Do all sorts for the young people, a club, an advice centre, run classes for women. They need it around here. Look at all those Bangladeshis in the streets. They need a Cultural centre, too, and maybe a language centre, as well. I could get funding, I'm pretty sure, if only I could get hold of the premises.'

'You've got the ideas all right,' said Jeff admiringly.

Toby blinked. If there was a crypt under the church, how come he'd not found it?

Nikki said, 'How do you get into the crypt?'

'You don't!' said their mother, short and sharp. 'There's a grille across and it's locked. I know. I got that churchwarden – much good he is – to let me have a look, but he says he's lost the key to the padlock! *If* you can believe him!'

'Standing in the way of progress,' bleated Jeff.

'It's the area!' said Kate, arms akimbo. 'Everything's just been left to rot. The people, the housing, everything. Look at all that graffiti! Typical!'

They all looked, with varying degrees of amusement and respect at Fats' latest offering, sprayed over a nearby hoarding.

'What does it mean?' said Nikki, interested.

'Never you mind!' said their mum, red in the face.

' "Kate and Jeff are . . .!" ' read Nikki. 'I can't quite understand the next two words.'

Toby grinned, but he wasn't really amused.

Jeff said, with a grand air of rising above the insult, 'Well, you can't expect anything else. It's the environment, and their rejection if it, their need to express their personalities, to perpetuate their . . .'

Toby wanted to laugh. All those fancy words. Fats liked painting, and he didn't like Jeff. That was all there was to it, really. And maybe their mum wasn't too popular, either.

'Sometimes I think,' said their mum, resolutely not looking at the message, 'that I'm never going to get through to these people. No back-up from the council . . .'

'Oh, come on!' said Jeff. 'You know I'm right behind you, all the way.'

Toby choked a bit. That was pretty much what the words on the hoarding meant. His mum blazed up.

'If I'd had one word of encouragement from anyone round here, I'd feel I wasn't wasting my time, but as it is . . .'

'What about the doctor chap? I've had some dealings

57

with him in the past. He's really caring, great influence within the local population.'

'Him! Oh, he's hopeless. My first impressions of him were the right ones. A proper old maid.'

Nikki said, 'How can he be "an old maid", if he's a man?'

'It's a saying,' snapped their mum. 'If a man's never been married, and acts prissy, he's called an old maid.'

'What's "prissy"?' said Nikki.

Before their mum could reply, a lorry came round the corner and swung a large skip through the gap in the hoarding, and on to the Wasteland. The doc rushed out of his surgery, and had words with the lorry driver, helping him to place the skip so that people could still get in and out, and the skip was clear of the pavement.

'Hi,' said the doc, grinning at them all. 'I've got the church people to agree to our cleaning the place up at last. I'll put a notice in my surgery, form a work party. The council will provide the skips for free, if we do the humping. Right?'

Kate and Jeff looked stunned. The doc picked up a rusty bike and threw it into the bottom of the skip with a satisfying clang.

'Got to rush back. Surgery full,' he said. 'Do a bit at a time. If you've got five minutes . . .? Just heave in what takes your fancy. See you!'

He rushed back into the surgery.

'What's "prissy"?' said Nikki, impishly. She might not have known precisely what it meant, but she'd got a good idea, all right.

Kate said something under her breath. She looked as if she were in shock.

'Well,' said Toby, trying not to grin too broadly, 'let's get started, shall we?' He picked up a black plastic bag and it burst, the contents tumbling yukkily all over his school trousers.

'Don't you dare!' said his mum. 'Leave all that stuff

where it is! It's really dangerous, a health hazard! I forbid you to touch it!'

'I thought you wanted the Wasteland cleared up,' said Toby. He hated the yukkiness on his trousers, which was beginning to seep through to his legs, but he could put up with it in a good cause.

'Yes, but it's not our job,' said his mum, pushing him out of the Wasteland. 'Come on, I've got to get those trousers in the wash straight away, if you're going to wear them to school tomorrow. Let the council clear the site. Or the church. The people who are paid to do it.'

'When there's no money . . .' said Jeff, not altogether agreeing with her. 'Perhaps if everyone did chip in . . .'

'Don't talk to me about Community Spirit!' said Kate, unfairly contradicting herself. 'It doesn't exist, round here. That skip will be full of other people's rubbish before nightfall, you see if it isn't!'

# 8

Toby hung out of his window and watched. He was supposed to be doing some homework, and then cleaning out his room, but this was far more interesting.

Fats came along, looked at the skip and walked all the way round it. He pulled out his spray can and signed his name on the side. Then he picked up some tin cans and threw them into the skip. He liked the sound of that, and did it again.

Skinny came round the corner and said, 'I can throw them further than you, I bet!' He backed off a bit, and threw some more in.

When Red came, they had a competition to find the bottles and smash them into the skip. Then they sat down to have a fag and talk about it. A couple of the others came by, kicked the skip, kicked a couple of bricks around, and talked about how their dad had a wheelbarrow and maybe they could borrow it, set up a plank, and walk stuff into the skip. They didn't do anything about it, though.

Mr Red came by, looking for his son. He looked at the skip, and he looked at the Wasteland, and he said maybe he could ask his boss about borrowing a dumper truck at the weekend. That would shift the rubbish, and no mistake.

A couple of motorists came by, saw the skip, reversed back to the entrance, got out, and dumped some of their own rubbish in it. A bloke came by with a junk lorry, came into the Wasteland and picked it over, looking for bits of metal. He took some of the bits out of the skip, and went off yelling 'Oh Aye!' which was probably meant to be 'Old Iron!'

After surgery the doc came out wearing an ancient boiler suit, and heavy gloves. He shifted some bits. Mrs Fats came along, with two of the younger boys, to find Fats. That was a sight, now! They got hold of this old settee, you couldn't sit on it, with all the cushions gone and the foam shredding out through the cover, and they heaved it up, all together, and it crashed down into the skip, and they all looked as if they'd done something really worthwhile. Which of course they had.

A man stopped to talk to the doc, and they sort of drifted around, arguing about this and that in a friendly way. Now and then they picked something large between them, and threw it into the skip. The churchwarden came by, said 'Humph!' or words to that effect, but didn't do any work himself. Perhaps he thought he was past it.

A couple of old women came by, leaning on their shopping trolleys. They stood and looked at the skip, and the land, and they stood and they stood. It would give them something to talk about for days.

In the morning there were a lot more bits and pieces in the skip, most of which hadn't come from the Wasteland.

Red said to Toby, 'That's not a bad table in the skip, and three chairs. We could use them in our Den.'

Toby didn't point out that they'd be late for school, but got to work helping Fats and Red pull the table and chairs off the skip and humping them into the church. The churchwarden kept the main doors locked, but somehow the lock on the side door just didn't catch properly – had it been tampered with Toby wondered – and you could easily get the door open if you knew how to jiggle it.

They stacked the stuff just inside the church and scarpered. It was worth getting a bad mark for being late, and anyway, someone would probably cover for them.

They hurried back to the skip that afternoon, and believe it or not, there was an old carpet there, thin and stained, but it would do nicely on the broken tiled floor. And there was Mr Red with one of his workmen, staring up at the windows of the church. Mr Red said that if the boys were going to get permission to use the church, he'd see what he could do about replacing the glass in the window.

'Permission?' Red and Skinny sort of grinned, and then made their faces go straight again.

They helped Mr Red and his workman to put ladders up against the church, and they held the bottom of them while measurements were taken. Mr Red poked and prodded at everything, taking notes, and saying they were lucky on the whole, there didn't seem much of a problem with the structure of the church itself, no new cracks, foundations OK.

He said he'd like to get down into the crypt to see if there was any water there, but the boys weren't going to admit they could get into the church unofficially, and anyway, they still hadn't worked out how to get through the padlock on the gate that blocked the stairs down to the crypt.

When Mr Red drifted off, pausing only to throw another plastic bag into the skip on his way out, the gang got themselves into the church. They swept the floor, sort of, and laid the carpet and the rug from upstairs. They put the chairs and the table on it, and thought it was great. They had cans of Coke, and some chips and some fags. Red put his feet on the table, showing he wasn't impressed by the fact that the building had once been a church.

Skinny, of course, was jerking up and down, worrying about how to get into the crypt. Maybe they could play five-a-side football down there, if it was big enough.

'No lights down there,' said Red, bringing out a pack of cards. 'Fancy a game?'

Fats had disappeared upstairs. Toby followed him. He didn't like the boys treating the church as if it were any ordinary sort of Den, but he thought he was being well, 'prissy', about it.

Fats was sitting on the bed, reading the old diary they'd found up there. He said, 'Hi. Wonder who this guy was. Musta been local. Seems he was a fire-watcher or something in the war, and this was his lookout. He musta felt sick when the church was bombed.'

Toby sat beside Fats, and they looked at some of the entries together. The diary dated back to the blitz. It wasn't a complete diary, not with dates for every day. Just notes, now and then. Like, 'Old Grey was killed last night, with all his family. Luckily the grandchildren are away in the country. He used to give us bulls-eyes, sometimes, when my mother wasn't looking. There's half his bed sticking out of the rubble. He was a good man. He was my Scout leader when I joined . . .'

'Mr Grey musta had a shop,' said Fats. 'Poor old man.'

'Scouts? Here?' said Toby. 'What happened to them?'

'Pfft. Went when the church went, I suppose.' Fats pushed the book away. 'Musta been quite different, then. No Bangladeshis, no block of flats, our school musta been small potatoes. We weren't here. Me dad come over from St Kitts in sixty-two, looking for work. Got work in the docks at first. Brought me mum over, we was all born here. When the work on the docks went, Dad got a job at sea, on an oil tanker. He's away months and months at a time.'

Toby had wondered about that.

Fats said, 'You gotta understand about me mum and church. She don't like me dad being on the tankers. She goes to the church and she prays and she brings us up the best way she knows, and she thinks that will keep me dad safe. I tell her that's superstition, but she can't help it. She says this isn't a proper church, and of course she's right.'

Toby said, 'It could be. It started off all right. All that with the doc, both Sundays, that was pretty good.'

'Sure. But look what's going on downstairs at this very minute. No respect. *They* don't think it's a church.'

'Why didn't you stay down with them?' said Toby, who had wondered how much Fats had been involved with the shadier doings of the gang.

'I don't, much. I never did. Some things I joined in. It was boring, being on me own so much. They never bothered me, if I didn't want to join in sometimes. Being big helps a lot.'

'. . . and being a Christian? How long have you been one?'

'Me mum would say "always". I'm not certain sure, myself. I sort of drifted into it. You can drift a long way without thinking what it really means. Then something happens, and you gotta do a bit of stock-taking.'

He looked at Toby, and gave him his wide, clever smile. Fats might not talk 'proper,' but he was very much all there.

Toby grinned back at him. Now they both knew where they stood.

Fats took out his spray can, sort of absent-minded, and was aiming it at one of the walls when Toby stopped him.

'Not in here, Fats.'

'I was only going to . . .'

'I know. But that don't make it right.'

Fats saw the point, even if he didn't like it. 'I could do a cross.'

'Do we need it?'

'Yes,' said Fats. And of course he was right, so Toby let him create a great big cross on one of the walls. It was an enormous cross, and Fats filled it in, doing the edges with care to make them sharp.

Then he snapped the can back into his pocket and

said, 'What I think is, this part of the world's a real dump. Our flat is clean because me mum works at it, but it's hard going, scraping and decorating all the time. Out of doors, you gotta take your chance. There's more muggings here than anywheres. Did you know Skinny's elder brother's in with that lot? Mike, that's his name. Yeah, well, Skinny don't talk about it much, but he is. Been sent away twice, now. You know what that means? The nick. Borstal. Training Centres. They got new names for them, but that's what they are. Now Mick's back, been back a coupla weeks, and that's why things have got worse. And they're not going to get better on their own, are they? So that's why we need the cross.'

'How can one cross on a wall here make any difference? No-one comes up here except us two, and Skinny once.'

'Two's enough, the doc said. We're the church. This room is the church. Wherever two of us are meeting to talk about Jesus. At least, I think that's what he meant.'

'But what can we *do*? Grown-ups won't listen to us, you know that.'

'Pray,' said Fats. 'Me mum would say we gotta praise God before we start asking for things. I've been thinking, what have we got to thank him for? This place, I suppose. The doc. Finding the Bibles here, so's we can read them when we want . . .'

Toby picked up one of the Bibles that had been left there, and flicked through it. Someone had marked a passage. His father had marked that very same passage, and it still didn't make much sense to Toby. What did Jesus mean when he said that either you were for him, or you were against him? Lots of people weren't bothered, either way.

He looked across at Fats, and thought how funny peculiar everything was. He'd been missing his old friends and his old school, and now he'd got Fats, and it looked as if they were going to be good friends.

Perhaps. If Fats felt the same way.

Fats looked up and smiled. Toby smiled back. It was all right. They were friends. Perhaps he could thank God for Fats. That would be a good start.

The echo of a commotion came floating up the stairwell. Fats and Toby went down. The air seemed to darken as they went down. It had been nice and light up in the tower room, but the church was dark. Some of the gang had been fighting. One of the chairs had been broken, and Skinny had blood running down the side of his face.

There were cards scattered around, and some money. Coke tins and chip papers and fag ends littered the place. It was a dump. It was like the Wasteland already.

The doc came in, carrying his bag. He said, 'Couldn't you have brought him to the surgery?' He pushed Skinny on to a chair, snapped at Red to hold the door open so's he could see what he was doing, and proceeded to mop up the damage. 'No stitches needed, you're lucky,' was the verdict.

He shut up his bag and looked around. Everyone shifted from one foot to the other.

He said, sounding tired, 'You know this is all wrong. You're trespassing. I know you haven't anywhere else to go. I am trying to get the authorities to let you have the run of the crypt, but if you break in here and make a mess, it's going to make it all the more difficult for me to persuade them. You do see that, don't you?'

Everyone looked down at the floor, and did a bit more shifting.

The doc said, 'And playing cards is OK, I suppose, but not gambling. And not in here, either. Do you read me?'

'Yes,' muttered Red. 'But me dad's going to put new glass in the windows, maybe help clean up inside. Then we could use it, couldn't we?'

'It isn't that.' The doc sat down, and motioned them

67

to sit down, too. 'Look, this neighbourhood isn't exactly Paradise, in spite of its name. I know how hard it is to keep straight around here. Sometimes it seems the only bit of fun you can get is by doing something against the law. I understand it, but that sort of thing is catching, like measles, and worse. Someone mugs an old lady and you blot out the terror and the hurt that she suffered, and you think, he came by the money easy. You almost get to admire the mugger. Then maybe someone asks you to act lookout for another rip-off, and they say, there's no harm in that, no-one can get you for it. So you do it . . .'

Toby thought, The doc knows all about Skinny and his brother Mike, and that's what he's talking about.

'. . . and maybe you don't get caught, and you get a hand-out, and you think Easy Money, why not help out again? And then maybe the next time you don't even get to worry about doing it, but just go ahead. And the third time you do the mugging yourself. Easy Money. Didn't cost you nothing, did it? Or maybe it did. Maybe it cost you your self-respect . . .'

'Gar . . .' said Skinny, shifting round some more.

'. . . or maybe it changed you in other ways. Because you can't afford to like people any more, can you? Not if you're thinking of doing them down.'

'What have they ever done for us?' said Skinny, putting up a fight.

'Fed, and housed you, Clothed you. Seen you got some schooling. Patched you up when you got into fights.'

Skinny changed colour. 'But I wouldn't . . . not you, doc. Nor anyone who, you know, not anyone like that.'

'Jesus said, "Either you're for me, or against me." You've got a choice. That's your right. That's what God gave you, the right to choose. It's up to you. You can stand firm and say "Get Lost" if you're asked to do something bad. Or you can say "it's only a little thing", and "what harm does it do?" And help the other side. Get it?'

Skinny got it. He nodded. He would have backed out of the door if he could.

Toby felt elation swell inside him. The doc had referred to the very passage that Toby had been puzzling over. So that's how it worked out in practice!

The doc hadn't finished with them, yet. 'Some of us are trying to make this better place to live in. It's hard going. Getting councils to do something about bad housing takes time and money, but we're working at it. Getting the streets cleaned up is another thing. That's something you can influence, you lot, for better or worse. And of course, there's the Wasteland to clean up.'

He smiled for the first time. 'The old skip's been taken away and a new one brought in. I've got the church people to agree we can use the Wasteland for a playcentre this summer, if we can clear out the rubbish. Do I hear any offers of help?'

'Yes,' said Red. 'If anyone else will.'

'OK,' said Skinny, and looked surprised at himself.

'Sure,' said most of the others, including Toby and Fats.

The doc looked round at them all, and each one of them felt the better for his approval. 'Right, then let's get this place locked up again, till we can get permission to use it properly. And take your junk with you, OK?'

The boys picked up their litter and drifted out, not happy about it, but ready to go along with the bargain. Toby and Fats hung back.

'Can't we even use the tower?'

'No,' said the doc, with regret but quite firm about it. 'You know you can't.'

Fats shrugged, and led the way out. Toby could read his friend's mind. They'd go along with the ruling in public, but they could always get in through the unblocked window if they wanted to. Toby squashed his conscience. It wouldn't do any harm, would it? And they might even do some good, by keeping watch for the baddies.

# 9

Then the most surprising thing happened. As they picked their way across the Wasteland, Kate Webb came towards them, smiling and waving at the doc! Everyone stopped to look at this extraordinary event.

'Marvellous news about the playcentre! I've just heard!' she said. 'I think I can swing a grant for a trained playleader, but I'll have to get onto it straight away . . .'

The doc stopped to talk to her. They were yakking politics, money, grants, left-wing this and right-wing that. Boring stuff. But the gang kept their ears open because you never knew, something interesting might come out of it. Not to mention the surprising sight of Kate Webb, who had advertised her poor opinion of the doc widely, actually smiling up at him, and helping him chuck stuff into the new skip.

'What a turn-up!' said Fats, which about expressed it for everyone.

Skinny, or one of his mates, brought in a big transistor, and they put on a tape, and got themselves organised with an old pram and a couple of planks to shift some of the smaller stuff. Nikki turned up with some of her friends, and they took over one corner and wouldn't let anyone else touch it. They said it was going to be their Den, so there!

Fats and Toby exchanged glances. Then Toby caught Skinny winking at Red, and Toby realised everyone had the same feeling about being shut out of the church. Technically it might not belong to them, but they felt, somehow, that they had a right! Even though 'right' wasn't exactly the appropriate word in the circumstances.

When it came to supper-time, the doc came upstairs with them, it being his half day off, and sat down just as he was, and stretched out his legs and offered to help with the cooking. Everyone laughed at that, but it turned out he lived all by himself now his parents were dead, in a house the other side of the estate, one of the bigger ones. He took lodgers in from time to time, because he liked company, and some of them had been students who needed a cheap place to live. Usually, he said, he cooked a huge pot of something twice a week and put it in the fridge, and heated bits up when he needed them. Stews, and jacket potatoes done in the microwave, lots of fresh fruit and he liked to try a new cheese every week, to see what it tasted like.

Toby couldn't believe his eyes, because there was his mum laughing and giving the doc some potatoes to scrub for the microwave, and asking him if he'd like a cup of coffee before the meal. She was acting just like she did with that awful chap Jeff. Toby sneaked a look at Nikki, to find her giving the doc one of her calculating stares. Nikki had a plan in mind to get something out of him. It didn't mean Nikki liked the doc. It just meant she was after something.

Money, perhaps.

Toby didn't like the thought of Nikki's taking advantage of the doc when he was off-duty, so to speak, and not expecting to be attacked. Toby felt protective towards the doc, and tried to frown Nikki out of whatever she had in mind. As much chance as seeing a local bus on Sundays.

'Mum,' she said, but looking at the doc as she said it, 'when we clear our patch, can we have a proper set of parallel bars, like the athletes on the telly?'

'Costs money,' said Kate, reaching for her ciggies. 'I'll have to see what the council budget has got left in it. Not much, I should think.'

'I doubt if we can put up anything permanent,' said the doc, 'because we've only got permission to use the place this summer.'

Nikki went right up close to him, and laid her hand on his knee. She had very intense blue eyes, just like her mum's. When she wanted to, she could charm birds off trees.

'But we need it!' she said, all honey and cream.

The doc flushed with pleasure. For one awful moment Toby thought he was going to give in, but he didn't. He laid his hand on hers. He put both his hands round hers, and held on to her while he looked back into her eyes.

'You've got all those things at school.'

'It's not the same,' she said, beginning to pout.

'No, I agree. Suppose you ask your mother if she can drum up a summer holiday scheme with *two* playleaders, one for the Wasteland, and one for the school sports hall? I know a couple of school governors, and I'll ask them to support the scheme.'

'We could do with two,' said Kate, waving smoke out of the way as she poured them some coffee, and stirred whatever she'd put in the saucepan.

'Your mother is one very powerful lady,' said the doc, passing the buck with a vengeance, and knowing exactly what he was doing. 'She'll fix it.'

'That's not what you said last week,' said Kate, stirring so hard she got red in the face. '"Tactless," is what I heard. "Crass". "Getting people's backs up!"'

The doc didn't duck it, but he got a bit red, too. 'Er, yes. Apologies. Perhaps we had got a bit set in our ways here. Do us good to be stirred up a bit.'

Nikki pressed up against him. 'I don't think you're prissy at all!'

'Nikki!' said her mother, angry and confused.

'Move along, Nikki,' said Toby. 'Help me set the table.'

Nikki made her innocent, big-eyed face, but went to

fetch the knives and forks. Toby thought the doc was amused, rather than angry. His mum was clashing pans around, red in the face. The doc was shaking. He began to laugh, and he laughed out loud. Toby grinned. The doc was a bit of all right.

'My stupid tongue!' said Kate. 'Sorry!'

'I like a good fight,' the doc said.

'Pax, then?' she said, just like a little girl.

'I've got a better idea. Join forces. OK?'

'Right,' she said, but she sounded as if she didn't know what she'd got herself into. Only Toby knew. He reckoned the outlook was set fair. Better than that old Jeff, any day.

'Trouble,' said Fats as they left school one afternoon. 'I've got to go round the First and Middle Schools, fetch the kids. Me mum was jumped on last night, coming back from the chippie. We get a treat, every Friday night, fish and chips from the chippie. She gets paid Fridays, you see. They got her purse, everything. But the worst is, she fell over on her ankle, and it's too bad to walk on. The doc says she's got to rest up. That means no going to work, and I've got to cart the kids to and fro, and do the shopping.'

'That's awful,' said Toby. 'I'll come round with you. Won't take much longer, and you'll need another hand with all those kids. What will your mum do for money, till she can go back to work?'

'She's got a rainy day box, and there's Dad's pay, in the post office. Don't spread it around that she's got a rainy day box, will you? We don't want a visit from the Bad Lads. She's got enough put by to see us through, probbly, with a bit of a stretch. Not worth going to the DHSS, and how would she get there, anyway, laid up as she is? You spend all day there and get the brush-off, even if you can afford the time. We'll manage, somehow.'

74

They walked along in silence.

Fats said, 'You didn't ask who done it.'

Toby felt his chest get tight. It hadn't got tight like that for ages, in fact, he hadn't even bothered to put his inhaler into his school bag for a couple of weeks.

'It probbly wasn't Skinny himself,' said Fats. 'Probbly. I mean, he does know my old mum. Had a meal with us once or twice. No, it was probbly his brother and a coupla their friends. Three of them, to get my old mum down and kick the bag out of her hand. They smashed the fish and chips packages, too, with their boots. At least they didn't smash her, after she was down. They might have, but they was wearing those ballyclavas, so she couldn't recognise them, not to be absolutely sure. Clever, that.'

'Where did it happen?'

'Down the alley between the chippie and the off-licence. You go straight onto the walkway and up to the flats from there. Usually there's people about, but just this once, zilch. She was on her knees, trying to get up, and they were way out of sight before anyone came along.'

'If we'd been up in the tower . . .'

'Sure, but we weren't. We wouldn't have been, anyway, not at that time of day.'

Toby felt dreadful. He went through his pockets and found one pound forty-five pence which he'd been saving up. He'd planned to take Fats and maybe Red, too, on a trip on the Docklands Railway, when his birthday came round. But this was more important. He pushed the money at Fats, who hesitated, but took it.

Toby said, 'Did she go to the police?'

Fats shook his head. No-one round there went to the police if they got mugged any more. Everyone knew who'd done it, but nobody could prove it. Once you were on the walkways up to the flats, you could skitter along, duck into a stairwell, come out the other side, hide in someone's flat, maybe. Or you could race along to the end of one walkway, and turn down the next one, and be in the middle of Paki-land before the cops got there. The cops did try. They'd practically camped out on Mike's doorstep for a while, but what could they do, if they couldn't catch him at it?

'It's got to be stopped,' said Fats, 'only I don't know how. It's getting worse. No-one's safe.'

'If we could get back into the tower, we could mount a watch, maybe, all over the weekends and after school.'

'So we see a coupla bods doing a job. They're wearing ballyclavas. So we watch them run away. That won't get us nowhere. Besides, we can't get back into the tower.'

They both knew they could, if they really wanted to. Only, the doc had sort of put them on the spot with his talk of helping the baddies by breaking the rules. They really didn't want to be against Jesus, not even in small ways.

'Got it!' said Toby, bringing them to a halt. 'We need a camera, like in banks and that. We see something, we snap it, we hand the proofs to the police. Right?'

'Haven't got a camera,' said Fats, trudging on. 'Besides, you'd need a really good one for that sort of thing. Distance, zoom lens. That sort of thing costs.'

'Yes,' said Toby. He still thought he'd got the beginnings of a plan there. If only he could get back up into the tower, he would have the whole area laid out before him, like a map. He could plan a campaign then, like a general moving his troops around. His mum had a camera. She might lend it, or she might not. Probably not. Nikki had borrowed it last year and lost the lens cap. Of course, Nikki hadn't asked permission to borrow it, first. Their mum had been fit to be tied, after.

He said, 'We could tell the police about the lookout, and they could put someone up there to keep watch with a good camera.'

Fats gave him the old heehaw. 'You're joking. By the

time the police got round to talking the church people into letting them use the place, it'd be Christmas!'

He was right, of course. Depressing.

# 10

Half-term was looming, and the cleared Wasteland was beginning to green over with weeds and wild flowers and even a shrub or two. The hoardings had been taken down for good, so that everyone could walk in and out as they chose. Some of the locals were coming in to have a nice sit-down on their way back from the shops. Sometimes Skinny and Red took along a couple of beaten up chairs and tried to charge the old people for sitting on them. Sometimes they got away with it.

No-one had yet gone back into the church. Toby had thought they would, but they hadn't.

Kate said that a lot of talk was going on among the church people, about the site. It had been left derelict for so long because the church people wanted to pull the tower down and build a new centre, or a block of flats or an old people's home or something. There hadn't been enough money for that, some of the high-ups had been agitating for a rebuilding job anyway, so the whole subject had died a death.

Now Kate was stirring things up again, wanting the use of the church crypt at least, and dry old men with accountants' eyes kept coming and looking at the place, with builders at their elbows, talking about the high cost of this and that, and going away again in posh cars.

Sometimes Kate was up in the air, thinking she was getting somewhere, and sometimes she was right down and reaching for the fags. The doc took them out to Greenwich one Sunday afternoon, and that was good. Another evening he took them to the theatre, and the following week on the river up to Tower Bridge and beyond. He and Kate were mostly good friends, though every now and then Kate would get mad at him, and then apologise and make up.

If she were in a bad mood with the doc, she'd say he was just like Toby's father.

Toby was old enough now to understand that this meant a lot. He knew all about loving somebody while being cross with their faults. He began to understand how it had been between his mum and his dad. For years he'd thought his mum must have disliked his dad – and therefore also disliked Toby – but now he realised she'd loved him a lot, and that's what had made her go raving bonkers when he'd died and left her alone.

Nikki tried on the charm with the doc, and when that didn't work very well, she sulked for a bit, and then decided it was a challenge and showed him her nice side. The doc liked her nice side. Toby could see him go all soft when Nikki curled up on his knee. But the doc saw through her little schemes, too, and he didn't let her get away with anything. Toby thought Nikki would go off the doc, when she couldn't wind him round her little finger, but that didn't happen, either. She was getting to respect him.

As for Toby and the doc, well, they'd always got along all right and that went on being more of the same and really satisfactory. They never argued, nor had to shout at one another. It simply wasn't necessary.

The Jeff character phoned up a couple of times. But Kate always said she was sorry, but she was busy. That was satisfactory, too.

The doc arranged to take them all out for the day on the Saturday at the start of the half-term holiday. Only there was an outbreak of chicken-pox, and he ran up to the flat to tell them he'd be late, and why didn't they go on without him.

Kate pulled a face. 'We can go another day. I've got so much work piled up, I'd just as soon get on with it, and maybe we can meet up this afternoon, go on the river or something.'

'I'll pop up if I get a chance, but I can't promise,' said the doc. 'Oh, and Toby, I forgot to tell you. Mr Red and his workmen are going to be in the church today, putting in new windows and seeing to the drainpipes, that sort of thing. I told him you'd keep an eye on things, see nothing goes missing while his back's turned. OK?'

'You mean we can go into the tower?' said Toby. The doc nodded. 'Mum, could I borrow your camera? I want to take some photos of the area from the tower.'

'Certainly not. You know what happened when Nikki took it, last time.'

'I've got an old banger of a camera you could borrow,' said the doc, cheerfully. 'It was my father's and I don't use it now, but it's got an excellent lens in it. Only takes black and white pictures, though. Will that do you? If so, you can come down and get it now and I'll show you how to use it. You'll have to get some new film. It hasn't been used for years.'

The camera was just the thing. It was old. It had a bellows front, and it was hard to master after their mum's point and click one, but the doc showed Toby some of its tricks, and told him which shop locally could give him the right film. The shop hadn't seen a working camera like that for ages, and some old boy tottered out to enthuse over it, and show Toby how to get distance shots in focus, and even loaded the camera for him.

This is it! thought Toby, as he hurried back to the church. 'The time, the place, the camera, and we've got permission to go up into the tower, so we're not breaking any promises.'

Fats was already at the church, with his brood. Skinny was there, and Red and most of the others. Also Nikki and her gang, who still wouldn't let anyone else into 'their' special corner.

Mr Red was inside the church, up a ladder. There

were several ladders there, and workmen were tearing down the old boards which had been hammered into place over the window frames. Light was in, and darkness was out.

Fats took one look at the camera and said, 'Ah-ha! And what have we here? Can I have a go?'

Toby got all his lot into a huddle and explained what he wanted to do. From the lookout they could keep watch on the alleys and walkways. The camera could be set up to photograph any suspicious movement down below.

Toby said, 'I'll operate the camera, so I'll have to be here most of the time, but I'll need help. We ought to work in pairs. Someone up here with me. A pair on the walkway to the right, and another pair maybe right up in the flats. The one with me here keeps watch with the binoculars, and keeps in touch with the others. Are you with me?'

They all looked at Skinny, who looked like he'd just died and forgotten to fall down.

Toby said, 'Skinny, do you want to opt out? You could just stay and help Mr Red, see none of their stuff is pinched. If you'd rather. We can see it might be awkward for you, if anyone you know is involved.'

Skinny opened his mouth, but no sound came out.

Fats said, 'Listen, he'll run and tell!'

Skinny shook his head, but still didn't speak.

'He won't tell,' said Toby. 'Will you, Skinny?'

'No,' said Skinny, recovering his voice and his normal colouring. 'I'm as fed up with this as you lot are. And so's me mum. We've tried talking to Mike, but you don't know what he's like. He scares me. And he's hit me mum twice already. If he's caught, if he's sent away for a long time, then I'll be glad. Right?'

'Right!' they all said.

'But we don't want him taking it out on you if he's caught,' said Toby. 'Why don't you take off for the day, maybe?'

'No, I'll stay and help. I know what clothes he wears, and what his friends look like. I can spot him quicker than you lot. I'll stay up here with Toby. If I see him leave our flat, I'll signal, somehow.'

'Yes, how?'

'Let me in!' said Nikki, furious at being excluded. She pushed through the boys and got into their midst, arms akimbo. 'I heard you, planning. I heard everything. You dare keep us out. I'll . . . I'll tell Mum on you!'

She was a chip off the old block, all right.

Toby said, peaceably, 'Well, all right. How do we signal, and what do our signals mean?'

'Anyone do Morse Code?' asked Nikki. 'No? Well, I don't either. How about towels? Or swimming things. I've got a bright red towel, and a blue swimsuit. We could hang them out of the tower window . . .'

'To show if the Baddies go left or right . . .'

'Port or starboard, it ought to be. Left and right. Red and Green.'

'Which is which?'

'I've got a green towel,' said Toby. 'If we hang that out, it means look to your left . . . that means our right . . .'

'Mix us up proper,' said Fats. 'Red means up towards the market, blue down towards the river . . .'

'And green is the alley. Most of the muggings are in the alley,' said Skinny.

Everyone thought, Well, he ought to know; he's probably been look-out for them a couple of times.

'What I think is,' said Toby, 'that whatever the signal might be, you stay where you are, and we stay where we are. We take the photos as best we can, and then we signal which way the Baddies take from . . . wherever. Up towards the market. Down to the river. Green for the alley. Then you lot have to watch out to see which way they go off. If they go back to Mike and Skinny's flat . . .'

Everyone looked at Skinny, who made a hissing, punctured tyre noise, but didn't speak.

'. . . then one person stays on lookout to make sure they don't go out again, and the other runs back here, and we go to the police with a report of what we saw. Anyone got a better idea?'

No one had. Skinny looked a bit sick and frightened, but he said someone would have to get him a burger for lunch, as he didn't intend leaving the church that day. He said it would be like an alibi for himself, just in case.

Nikki sped off to collect towels and her blue swimsuit, and marshal her own troops. They selected a pitch for themselves outside the post office near the alley. They set themselves up with a transistor radio on the pavement, which meant that one or other of them would always be able to keep an eye on the end of the alley. Who would think of expecting trouble from a bunch of girls hanging around a transistor radio on a pavement? Unless you knew Nikki, that is.

There were plenty of people about. It was, after all, a Saturday, and what's more, it was the first Saturday for a long time that the weather had been half-way decent. It was warm enough to go out without a jacket. Everyone and his wife were out in the streets, shopping, nattering, giving the children what for if they got underfoot. A normal, busy day.

'They'll never come out in this,' said Toby. 'Surely they'll wait till things quieten down a bit.'

'You mean we might not get them today?' said Skinny. 'I couldn't go back home. He'd know, as soon as he set eyes on me. It's got to be today.'

Nikki and her lot took it in turns to go home for lunch. She brought Toby up something to eat, and said her mum was so busy on the phone that she'd hardly noticed the children weren't around.

Fats climbed the tower to say he'd been looking after

his brothers all morning, and was worn out. He was doing the shopping after lunch, and then would come along to help.

Time passed, and nothing of any importance happened, except that Red dropped out of the roster for a while, to help guard his dad's ladders.

'They gotta do it today!' said Skinny.

It would all fall apart if they didn't get some action that day. Toby knew he'd never get the others to keep on, day after day, on the off-chance. He rubbed his eyes, which were sore from peering into dark corners. He had taken a couple of photos, just to get the feel of the camera, but he didn't dare waste too much of his film though he was beginning to feel that it might not be a bad sort of hobby to take up, if he had some spare time in the future.

'Come on, come on!' said Red, who had popped up to see what was happening.

Skinny said, 'If they don't come out, what do we do?'

'We can't give up so soon,' said Toby.

Still nothing happened, except that one of Mr Red's workmen nearly fell off a ladder and broke the pane of glass he'd been carrying. That would take some clearing up.

Skinny abandoned the binoculars, and started reading the old diary, hunching himself up on the bed in the corner. Fats came up, with some good news. His mum was hobbling around with a stick now, and a neighbour had offered to take the youngsters swimming that afternoon.

Toby ached all over from having to sit still.

Fats poked Skinny. 'What's that you got there?'

'Diary,' said Skinny, in a bad mood. 'Chap who was air-raid warden here. Lookout man for bombs and fires. Me dad said his dad used to be one, too. Worked all day, and watched all night. They was bombed out, like this guy.'

'I didn't know that,' said Toby, raking the alley for the umpteenth time with his glasses. 'What happened?'

'Dunno. He just says. His wife was OK, but the house went. I expect they were rehoused in the flats, like our lot, after the war. Prefabs first, and then they built the block and moved everyone into it. Me dad used to say everyone thought the flats were wonderful, at first. That didn't last long.'

Skinny held the book up. 'This chap says he could see the City burning from end to end. He says he was too tired to be frightened. He says the important thing was never to give in. He was talking about Hitler making everyone live in fear.'

Fats said, softly, 'We could pray about that. In the name of Jesus. He is here, and knows everything that's going on. He knows we're trying to stop the bullying, and the hurting and the evil. Please, Jesus, help us.'

'Amen,' said Toby. 'We can't go it all by ourselves, Jesus. We need you to help us.'

'I'll go along with that. Maybe,' said Skinny, 'I ought to say, too, that I'm sorry that I helped them before. I didn't see no harm then.'

Fats went to take up his station with Red, who was reading a comic, high up on the walkway.

'I'm getting bored with this,' said Skinny. 'And I'm hungry. The shops are shutting. People are going home. Nikki's gone to sleep, I think. How much longer do we have to hang around?'

'We don't,' said Toby, who'd been having another go with the binoculars. 'I think that's them leaving your flat now!'

# 11

Skinny grabbed the glasses. 'Yes,' he said. 'That's them, all right. Me brother Mike, and two of his mates. Lewis, that's the big black bloke. The other's Ricky, that my brother was at school with.'

'Quick! What do they look like?' said Toby. 'Are they wearing balaclavas?'

'They're coming down the walkway, all three of them, taking their time. No hurry. They're all smoking. No balaclaves.'

'Not out for blood, then.'

'Fats has signalled with the blue. They're turning off towards the river. They're going to the pub, probbly.'

'Pub's only just open. Are they flush with money?'

'Dunno. Not sure. They said they were going to do some betting on the races today. No, they've gone past the bookies. They musta lost.'

'If they lost, they may be on the lookout for some easy money.'

'Yes,' said Skinny, sort of strangulated.

The tension was getting to Toby, too. He took a photo of the three men standing outside a pub. They were still taking it easy, arguing a bit, but not in any hurry about anything.

While Skinny kept his eyes to the glasses, Toby hung a blue costume out of the window. Below him, Nikki suddenly woke up and looked alert. She and her friend began to play hopscotch. It showed a certain lack of imagination, that it had to be hopscotch. Normally Nikki wouldn't be seen dead, playing hopscotch.

'They're off again,' said Skinny. 'Can't see where. Out

of sight behind the buildings.'

There was a painful stretch of time when nothing happened. The blue signals stayed out. Nikki hopscotched like mad. Fats and Red craned over the edge of the walkway.

'They've gone off somewhere for the evening,' said Skinny. 'It's not going to work. Your mum will want you for supper soon, won't she?'

'Mm,' said Toby. 'Just give it five minutes more.'

He focussed the camera on the alley. There was an interesting shadow across it now. Black and white, he'd heard, could be even better than colour. A shot like that might be well, dramatic.

Into the alley crept an old bundle of a woman, dragging her basket on wheels. The basket was almost full of empty bottles. She was on her way to the Off-Licence.

Toby knew her. It was the same woman who'd almost been mugged in that alley, the very first time he'd looked. She should be safe this evening, though.

'Old Miss Stein, going for her gin,' said Skinny. 'Did you see all those gin bottles? You wouldn't believe she could get through so much, would you?'

'But gin costs!'

'She's got plenty. A brother in America sends her, regular, and she has a pension from the company she used to work at. She's a neighbour of mum's, keeps herself to herself.'

'They nearly mugged her before when I was watching. They must know she's not skint.'

Skinny shrieked. 'It's Fats! It's green! They've come back, and they're going down the alley!'

Toby rushed to hang out the green, take in the blue, and get back to the camera. They could have done with a third man.

Nikki was looking up at them, her face blank in the sunlight. Miss Stein continued to crawl down the alley, putting all her weight on one foot and then shifting to the other. Her feet hurt her, you could see.

Toby wound the camera on, and clicked the shutter open. And wound on again.

'Green, green, green!' chanted Skinny, jogging up and down. 'Come on, come on!'

'There!' Into the shadows at the back of the alley moved three dark figures. Denims, sweaters, T-shirts, all as before. Balaclavas, that was new. They looked like soundless spiders, shadowing the old woman.

Click! Toby clicked and wound on again. How many more exposures did he have? The three moved into the light. Click!

No, there were only two of them. One had stayed behind, watching the far end of the alley. Lookout man. Thank God it wasn't Skinny, this time.

The big coloured bloke shouldered past the old woman, throwing her off-balance against the wall. She fell in a flurry, all fat arms and legs. Her basket tipped over and there was a soundless tinkle of glass as some of the bottles fell out and broke.

'That's Lewis. Do they know where she keeps her money? Yes!'

Click! went the shutter. The coloured bloke stood over the woman, and as she tried to get to her feet, he kicked out at her, quite casually. She lay where she'd fallen, mouth open, stunned or winded or just too scared to move.

There was no-one else coming down the alley, yet. Nikki was glued to the wall, peeping around. And her mate behind her, biting her nails.

Someone was coming, a couple, arms around one another, heads together. They stopped right by the entrance to the alley. They hadn't caught on, yet, what was happening there.

Skinny's brother tipped the basket right over, and scrabbled around, sending bottles this way and that. He raised his arm with a brown purse in it.

Click!

'They're off, back the way they came!' Skinny pulled in the green, and waited, waited, holding the glasses up with one hand. 'Which way? Come on, Red; come on, Fats!'

'Blue!'

'Towards the river? No. Fats is signalling again, taking it in. He's turned his back on us, talking to Red. What's going on?'

'They've gone up the walkway, that's what. Going past them, can't you see? Taking their ballys off as they go.'

'Click!' But Toby wasn't sure he'd moved quickly enough to catch the moment when the trio took their balaclavas off.

'Fats and Red are following, slowly. Careful! Don't get too close! Lewis is in the lead. Up the first stairwell. I've lost them. They've gone inside somewhere. Not our flat.'

They waited. Nikki and her friend sped along the walkway, and joined Fats and Red by the stairwell. Nikki disappeared. After a little while, all four of them came running back, Nikki racing ahead. She came panting up the stairs and flopped on the bed.

'I followed them, all the way. They never noticed!'

Fats and Red came in, with Nikki's mate. They were all out of breath.

'Where did they go?'

'They went into flat number sixty-three,' said Nikki, trying to get her breath back. 'You can't see it from here. Fats and Red followed them to the stairwell, but I went right in after them. I knew they wouldn't take any notice of me, and they didn't. They were laughing. They stopped on the landing outside No. 63, ringing the bell. No-one came at first, so they were laughing, talking about what they'd just done. They split the money there and then, while they were waiting to be let into the flat.

They said it was a nice purse, might do for some girl or other, Ann something. Lewis got to keep the purse. If we hurry, we can get the police round there while they've still got the money and the purse!'

# 12

The police were very pleased with them. The photos proved everything beyond a doubt. Toby had caught the Baddies before and after they'd put their balaclavas on. He'd caught Lewis pushing the old woman, and he'd caught Mike holding her purse in the air after. When the police walked in on the Baddies, they found the purse still in Lewis' pocket, together with Miss Stein's pension book, and her money. That clinched it, and Nikki was told, to her annoyance, that she would not be needed to give evidence.

The local press picked it up. Toby was late getting back from school on the day the reporters called. So Nikki obliged, instead. She gave them an interview, and posed for a photo, too.

The doc brought Toby in a copy of the local paper. There was Nikki on the front page. 'Hawkeye of Paradise Row', was the headline. The story was all about Nikki and how clever she'd been to track down the Baddies. It hardly mentioned Toby.

On the next page there was a photo of Kate Webb, triumphantly waving a football in the air.

'Holiday Spree for All,' said that headline. The story was about Kate having got holiday schemes approved by the council, one for the school sports hall, and one for the Wasteland.

The doc looked at Toby, with an odd sort of smile. Toby felt miffed. Distinctly miffed. Then he began to laugh, and the doc began to laugh, too.

Toby said, 'You had as much to do with the council agreeing to the scheme as she did.'

'We're the powers behind the thrones, don't you think?'

The doc looked quite happy about it. Toby relaxed. He didn't feel so bad about it now. He was even able to smile. Trust those two!

The doc was teaching Toby how to play chess. Nikki said it was a mug's game, and maybe she'd learn later, but just now could the doc help her make a really big kite that she could fly from the church tower. The doc had got permission for a community centre to be run from the church crypt, and he'd also got permission for a holiday supervisor to use the church itself when it rained. Mr Red and his workmen were making the place safe, and putting in some new wiring for lights down in the crypt.

'And will it be a proper church again on Sundays?' Toby wanted to know.

'Maybe,' said the doc. 'I'm working on it.'

Kate came in with coffee for herself and the doc. She seated herself, one leg under, and leaned back.

'Phew, it's been a long day. Did you see the piece in the paper about the Holiday Schemes?'

'You're doing just fine,' said the doc. He took the coffee and looked around him. 'It seems odd, being here again. Back to one's beginnings, and all that. We used to live here, you know, till my father died, and then I bought my present house, so's my mother didn't have to climb the stairs.

'Have your family always lived around here?' said Kate.

'Yes, my grandfather said he couldn't live anywhere else. He had a little workshop down the road, making fancy buttons. I'll show you some of his buttons, sometime. The workshop's gone now. Bombed. They just moved into the next street and got on with it. He was a character. I think he influenced me even more than my own father. I suppose because he had more time to spend with me. He had an allotment . . . but that's all gone now, too.'

'We ought to bring back allotments,' said Kate, 'and private gardens.'

'He had a garden, too. A scrap of ground, but it grew so many roses, you couldn't count them all. Grandad was gassed in the first world war, limped a bit, worked longer hours than anyone around. He was churchwarden here, you know. And bellringer in chief. He loved the place. I think it broke his heart when the church was bombed. He kept saying to me, and my dad, 'They'll rebuild, one day. They can't get us down! We'll have to get organised, make them rebuild.' The doc grinned at Kate. 'Sounds like the sort of thing you say, Kate.'

'Nothing gets done around here unless you push,' said Kate. 'You see, they didn't rebuild, did they?'

'No, well, he hoped my dad would be politically minded, carry on the fight, but it didn't work out that way. My dad had been in a prison camp in the Far East. He wanted to be a doctor. It was hard, starting to train to be a doctor in his late twenties. He wasn't married, then, of course, and money was tight. When he did get married I came along straight away, and my mother went out to work as a typist to help out, so I spent a lot of my time with my grandparents. I used to play with his tin hat and gas mask. He was the air raid warden at the church here, till it was bombed.'

Toby thought, So that's who the diary belongs to! It was the doc's grandad! I wonder if it was him I saw in my dream. Mum would say that was nonsense, but I don't know so much. It certainly started something.

As soon as the doc had gone, Toby went next door, through the newly-levelled entrance into the Wasteland, past the stumps of masonry where perhaps there would be roses growing one day, and past the piles of tree trunks and planks which would be the new Adventure Playground equipment. He poked his head round the door which led down to the crypt. It was still dark and smelly down there. Toby went up into the church proper, and found it all light and clean and newly swept. It looked very empty. He wished Fats were there, or even Skinny, so that they could fill it with prayer again.

But the time wasn't ripe for it. Not yet.

He went up the stairs to the lookout.

It was a beautiful day, just right for flying kites. Nikki had been up there, he could see, because she'd left her half-made kite on the bed. She wasn't there now. There wasn't anyone there.

He rescued the diary and the binoculars. He'd take them down and show them to the doc. The doc was taking them all out to McDonald's for supper that night. Good for the doc.

Toby leaned on the window, letting the sun get at him. It was good up there, drowsy in the sun. He closed his eyes.

When he opened them again, he was looking straight across at the flats.

He began to laugh. Fats had been at it again. Everyone would know who had done it. Toby wondered how Fats had managed it without killing himself. There'd be trouble. You weren't supposed to go around defacing buildings like that.

Toby got his binoculars out, and the message leaped into view.

JESUS LIVES, OK.